Make Me

By Rhiannon Holte

Make Me contains references to pictures of Anya, Rhiannon, and the rest of the inner circle doing the makeovers voted on by the fans. If readers want to see the pictures, please visit the website www.makemeover.us and click on the "Media" tab on the menu. Click on "Pictures" to see Rhiannon's Production Diary for the project or click on "Ria's notes" to see a list of the images in the order that they appear in the book. Feel free to check out the rest of the website for additional information on the people behind this website and the fans who made it a phenomenon.

*This book is for
Maren, the sister I lost,
and Anya, the friend
I hope I will never lose.*

Chapter 1

The Trial Run

Like most of us, Anya Allen knew that beauty is the fairy dust of fate. She also knew that if a girl wanted to be a star, she would need something more precious than beauty, something rarer than talent. She needed luck. And if that girl was a former child television star who had earned a reputation for being "difficult," she would need a miracle. Or at least her own YouTube channel.

Anya's TV show, *Extra Points,* was about a group of gymnasts learning lessons about friendship and competition that parents don't have time to teach—kind of like *Glee* but with uneven bars. Anya played a ten year old who rocked the balance beam and America loved her, but by the time she turned 14 the show was cancelled, and Anya fell through the cracks of Hollywood Boulevard. While she tried to find her next thing, she did what most kids too young to be famous do—she picked up a DUI, went out with jerks, and let those vampire types who bleed celebrities dry have their way with her.

According to the magazines, when she did get work, she came in late and mouthed off to directors. At seventeen, her career was practically dead; producers hired her in case the audience wanted an update on the wreckage. She'd even accepted a few infomercials, drinking antioxidant shakes that looked like puke and doing those seven minute workouts for hard abs. By the time I met her, she was working at H------ to pay for acting classes. I was eighteen, a recent escapee from Connecticut, and ready to start over. H------ trained us both on the same day, if you could call it training; they barely gave you a chance to learn the computer system before throwing you on the floor. It's every girl for herself in that cathouse, but somehow we became friends.

Maybe we got along because we were the same age or maybe it was because I was one of the few waitresses there who didn't dream about being in the spotlight. Secretly I hoped when my parents heard I was working at H------, it would shock them back to life like those paddles paramedics use to get someone's heart beating. But when I told them it didn't make a dent. I could've been working at a book store.

Anya needed to make a change or accept the depressing reality of living a normal existence; it must be hard to deal with the fact that the most exciting moments of your life are in the past. That's how she came up with the idea behind *makemeover.us*. (We couldn't afford the .com or the .net. It would've cost about $1800, which was a lot to us back then.) Looking back, what's amazing is not that it brought in millions of fans in six weeks—it's that we didn't try to stop it sooner. But in the beginning, when there were about one hundred thousand people following the website, many of them diehard fans of *Extra Points*, it seemed that lightning had decided to strike twice. For once, Anya's destiny wasn't in the hands of some casting agent with a French manicure.

Three months after our first day, she quit H------ and convinced me to go along for the ride as associate producer for the site. Our first step was to find some start-up money, so Anya asked this assistant cameraman she knew, Javier, to help us put a video up on *Kickstarter*, if people like what they see they donate money and if the project gets enough donations, you get to keep the money. I don't think about the last few days of the website unless I've doubled down on my Lexapro, but in the beginning it was fun. And exciting. And soooo cool.

From the hips up Anya looked like a ballet dancer with narrow shoulders, small boobs, muscular arms—but from the hips down she had the round firm butt and powerful legs of a Latina. (I say "looked" because that was before the fans got a hold of her.) Back when she was on *Extra Points*, she had to practice about three hours a day and keep her weight under 105 pounds; it was in her contract. I don't know what all that exercise and dieting did to her, but from the time she was ten she learned that her body was a tool you could mold like Playdoh.

She has big hazel eyes and lips that are full but not scary thick like some actors I will not mention. You'd think anyone who had been in the acting business since second grade would know how to dress to make the most of her looks, but Anya had zero fashion sense, which didn't help her in auditions. She had this thing for—I don't even know what to call them-- jumpsuits? rompers?

She liked to wear them because they were easy, and she didn't have to think about matching anything. For Anya, it was all about how quickly she could get ready rather than what she actually wore. She'd brag that she could shove her hair in a bun and get out the door in under fifteen minutes. [Picture of Anya hanging out in one of her rompers (mm1ab)] The only problem is that it looked like all she took was fifteen minutes, which is fine for a guy but doesn't work out so great for a girl, especially one who wants to make a comeback. (The first thing I did once the site started making money was max out my credit card on clothes and makeup because I knew that for once I could pay it off.) This is what gave her the idea for the website. She knew she needed to reboot her life and the best way to do that was with a complete makeover. Why not give that job to somebody else and maybe get some media attention along the way? Anya came up with four basic rules for the site. Unfortunately, as her new associate producer, I came up with number five.

Makemeover.us

The Big Five

1. At the beginning of the week, a category would be announced. Examples included hair style, clothing, tattoos, piercings, etc.
2. Fans would have 24 hrs. to upload makeover tips to the website *makemeover.us*. After 24 hrs., the makeovers would be frozen. Fans would then have 48 hrs. to vote or "Like" their favorite makeover.

3. The suggestion with the most "Likes" would win. A video of Anya doing that makeover would be posted on the site and our YouTube channel—if it was clothing for an event, she would be taped trying on the clothing and going to the event; if it was a tattoo, footage of Anya getting the tattoo would be posted, etc.

4. If at any time, Anya chose not to adopt a winning makeover, the website would be terminated.

5. Every four weeks fans would be allowed to come up with the category. After 24 hours, fans would be able to vote for the category of their choice. Once the category was selected, the fans would have 24 hrs. to upload their makeover tips as usual. Anya would have 24 hours to decide whether she would accept the winning makeover or terminate the project.

Week One

Javier wasn't just good with a camera, he was also a major computer nerd. He made us an awesome website and created a free app that featured an avatar of Anya. When I first met him I thought no way would he be any good because he definitely didn't look like somebody who spends hours in front of a computer screen, but it turned out that he knew what he was doing. He lived with his parents (he was saving up for this Epic Red camera and some Diva lights) who rent half of this cool brownstone with a little workout room in the basement; he and his buddy Austin practically live down there when they're not shooting something. The way I see it, the only thing that's fun about working out is distracting someone else from working out. [Pictures of Javier and me working out. (mm2abc)] [Would it kill him to eat a donut? (mm2de)]

Getting back to the site's Apps, users could dress Anya up, change her hair and make-up, give her piercings, pretty much anything. We put up a video on YouTube of Anya explaining the rules and Javier made it so that as she talked her appearance changed—different hair, clothes, piercings, tats—it got the point across that she was willing to be a work in progress. For the first category we played it safe with a "Hair Makeover" and fans uploaded all kinds of images. Back in those days the fans bought into the spirit of the site, which was about helping Anya get her life together.

After 24 hours they voted and the winning makeover had 11,799 likes, which wasn't bad for a first week. We filmed her going to a salon and getting her hair cut and dyed black. [Pics of Anya at the salon (mm3ab)] Anya's original hair was pretty—kind of a light brown and really long—but the fans thought she should go for a more dramatic look, and I have to say that they were right. The new hairstyle made her look more like a woman, less like a girl, which is what she needed if she was going to be taken seriously as an adult actor. [Pic of Anya's new look (mm4c)] At the time we felt like it validated the project and we were really psyched!

Chapter 2

The Audition

Week Two

Anya was auditioning for Mary Epstein, who is a big agent in New York and takes on new clients like almost never. It was an important opportunity, so we asked the fans what she should wear. The dress they picked wasn't half bad, simple so that it didn't distract from Anya, and tight enough so that it showed off her figure. She wasn't crazy about the idea, but I convinced her to wear a push-up bra. I thought that Anya had to remind that agent that she was no longer a child actor—she was a woman with a kick-ass body. After the vote, Javier filmed her going to the audition and doing her monologue. [Pictures of Anya heading out to the audition in her new dress—43,400 Likes (mm4ab]

She didn't end up landing Epstein, which actually turned out to be a good thing because losing increased Anya's likability. The fans had chosen her dress and her hairstyle; therefore, her rejection was their rejection. They left tons of sympathetic comments on the website and blasted Twitter with horrible digs about Epstein (who come to find out is actually really nice. Sorry Mary!). According to Google Analytics, this was when *makemeover.us* started to get some traction—it wasn't just the interactive quality of the project, it was their connection to Anya as an underdog. People are great about offering second chances as long as they think the person has suffered enough.

Chapter 3

Ink

Week Three

Letting someone else pick your tattoo is a major deal because tattoos usually express something very personal. On my seventeenth birthday I got a tattoo of Goofy; I was supposed to wait until I was eighteen to make that kind of *major life decision*, but I was going out with this guy who worked in a tattoo place. [Pictures of me and Miguel kicking back in my old room (mm5abc)] He did mine after hours, and my parents never said a word about it. Most normal parents would've freaked out when they saw their daughter with a dude who was obviously much older, but of course they didn't.

A lot of people, if they see my tattoo, probably judge me as immature, but I don't care. Goofy reminds me of Disney World which was the last vacation my family took before my older sister Maren died. We booked a special breakfast at the hotel; the characters would visit your table and joke with the kids and let families take pictures. I have lots of pictures with a whole bunch of the characters, but my favorite is the photo Goofy took of me and Maren sitting at the table with pancakes shaped like Mickey on our plates and my sister holding two fingers behind my head like devil horns. [Pictures of me and Maren goofing around at breakfast (mm6)] That morning I remember thinking that my sister was a lot like Goofy—tall and gangly with pointy elbows and good intentions. After that trip, everything changed; we tried to keep the old rituals—decorating the house for Halloween, buying a Christmas tree, stuffing the turkey--but it was an empty performance. Eventually, we had to sell the house to pay the legal and medical bills. After I got my diploma, my parents moved to Florida to bury themselves in a retirement community; it took them a while to have kids, so they just made the minimum age requirement. Dad still does some taxes on the side; I don't know what Mom does to stay busy.

Which brings me back to my point: tattoos should tell a story or they are a waste of ink. We decided to have Anya open up and talk about herself on camera, provide fans with a *Cliff's Notes* version of her life since rehab. (Most people had a pretty good idea of what happened before rehab.) One of the things she told the fans was that she was trying to treat her body like it was a gift rather than a playground—no drugs, no cigarettes, alcohol only on special occasions. She was also a pescatarian, which meant that she still ate fish and eggs (as long as she didn't have to crack the shells open). Maybe you have to go through withdrawal to make those kinds of changes in your life. I believe your body is definitely your playground and you should have as much fun as you can with it in case somebody bulldozes it away.

The tattoo makeover turned out awesome because the fans chose this Celtic Tree of Life design (189,267 Likes). [Picture of the winning design (mm7a)] Some of the fans voted for it because Anya is big on the environment and some because of her Irish background. (Fun Fact: Anya is an old Irish name that means "radiance." It goes back to Aine, who was a fairy queen and one of the wives of Fionn Mac Cool! No kidding!). She is supposed to be lucky in love (not so far) and in money (fingers crossed!). My mother named me after one of her favorite songs from the 70s. Why she thought it was a good omen to name her baby girl after a woman who is always flying away and leaving people broken hearted, I have no clue. We did include one rule—no tat on the face or neck because Anya needs to be marketable as an actor. The fans chose the back of her right shoulder, which is definitely a cool spot with the branches stretching up and almost reaching her shoulder and the roots of the tree trailing down towards her back. Anya squeezed my hand until I thought my fingers would break, but we got it done. [Pictures of Rob giving Anya the tattoo (mm8abc)]

Usually we get a few wacky makeover tips, but two of the images that were uploaded in the first 24 hours were creepy. One was a swastika and the other was a sketch of a needle dripping blood into a spoon, which if you ask me was definitely a mean reference to the rumors about her addiction to heroin. Anya said she never got into it, but who knows? She went to rehab for something. Obviously they didn't receive a lot of votes, (231 Likes for the swastika and 92 for the needle) but it was disturbing that they got any Likes at all. I didn't want to think about some white supremacist dressing Anya's avatar up in a Nazi dominatrix uniform. Not that she didn't have experience being the object of male fantasy both while she was on television and during her short stint at H------. The first thing a pretty girl learns is not to think about what a guy might be thinking about.

Once we hit a million unique users, it was ridiculous. That's when the fans developed their own YouTube channel and uploaded confessional video clips explaining why they voted the way they did. At first it was fun to get a visual of what our fans were like and hear what they were thinking, but after a while it got weird. Some of the fans seemed too obsessed with Anya, and I started wondering if we should hire a few bodyguards, but Anya said no. She says that bodyguards turn into prison guards real fast. There was this one lady, Georgia127, who was a conspiracy theory type. She'd play the videos and pause them, claiming to find mysterious edits or evidence of green screens: The tattoo parlor wasn't real or the hair cut was a wig. And there was this tranni, @mebecraze, who vowed to do every makeover Anya adopted. [[Picture of @mebecraze wearing the exact same dress as Anya (mm9a)] She needs some serious help with that wig!

Chapter 4
Fans' Choice

Week Four

According to the rules, it was time for the fans to pick the category and they were ready. The winning choice was "Plastic Surgery" and the winning makeover was breast implants. Back at H------, every once in a while a random guy would say something dumb because she didn't have the typical cup size. One customer asked if she was their Affirmative Action hire, but she never let it bother her. She said that women with big boobs were often typecast as stupid, as sluts, or as stupid sluts. Anya sort of considered herself a feminist. I know that seems crazy for a girl who worked at H------, but we all make our compromises along the way.

When the fans chose breast implants, Anya had her first doubts about the project. All those hours of practice molding her body into a hard flexible strip of muscle—adding two bags of saline to her chest would throw everything off. Plus, it's one thing to wear a push-up bra, it' another to go under the knife. On their YouTube channel, the fans argued that finding roles that didn't involve getting naked or at least showing some major cleavage would be pretty tough. *HBO* and *Showtime* pretty much specialize in soft porn, but along with all that sex are some great series with cool parts for women. They weren't talking Double Ds, and they seemed to be thinking about what was best for Anya's career.

Here was the big moment—accept the makeover or shut it down and go home because if Anya didn't do it, our website would be no different from any other reality show. According to the rules (as more than one fan reminded us) Anya had 24 hrs. to make her decision. Traditional media was pounding on our door: we received lots of requests for interviews after the surgery—morning shows, the late nights, *People, In Touch, HuffPost*. Not everyone approved of the concept behind the website. Some of those media "experts" thought we were headed for trouble and compared us to the Stanford Prison Experiment. I just finished a Psych 101 course online so I knew what they were talking about. Comparing our site to a horrible study that turned a bunch of college kids into sadists was stupid, but I guess pundits have to make their money somehow.

Before my sister died, there was no question that we would both go to college—my mom was a guidance counselor and my dad was an accountant. Maren played basketball and it looked like she'd probably get offered a few scholarships. Her first choice was UCONN because a lot of her friends were there, and they had a really good team, I guess. I think of my childhood as split into two periods—*Before The Accident* (**BTA**) and *After The Accident* (***ATA***). In the ***ATA*** period, my parents decided I'd be better off homeschooled. I guess they wanted to spare me having to walk through the halls of our high school and hear the whispering about my family. I didn't argue with them. I was afraid that around every corner I'd run into Heather in her wheel chair. I took classes on my laptop from an accredited program and got my diploma three months after my seventeenth birthday.

What surprised me was my parents never pushed college, never even brought it up. You'd think they would've been even more determined to have me go given that my sister never would, but despite my almost straight A's, they couldn't even think about it. We didn't visit campuses, didn't get a seat for the SATs or fill out applications. No senior prom, no graduation party, I got a job at a Friendly's in a nearby town and dated boys who never heard of Maren. I took online college courses so that my brain wouldn't turn into mush in case my parents woke up from their comas and decided I could use a future.

When I turned eighteen, I asked my dad if he could spot me some money for the security deposit on an apartment in New York. He said yes and I guess they felt that with me gone there was nothing left keeping them in Connecticut, so they packed up my childhood in boxes marked **Florida** or **Charity**. We became a family of pretenders; we changed our addresses and pretended to move on but we were still stuck in the past.

The fans' choice of implants was the first time we seriously considered what Anya's end of the deal was. *Makemeover.us* doubled its number of unique users and those fans had become an intimate part of Anya's life. Letting others choose your hair style or clothing is one thing—letting them change your body is another. But the rewards were right there; we'd already started making some serious money from ads on

YouTube and the website. When we went out to a restaurant or club, we got the VIP treatment because somebody on the staff was a fan. Anya was used to signing autographs and getting random calls from other celebrities asking her to hang out from her days on the series, but I was blown away. Nevertheless, she was the one going under the knife so the big question was—how bad did she want another shot?

I haven't mentioned it yet but Anya had a boyfriend named Jake. They broke up and made up so often I never knew whether he still qualified as her boyfriend or not. She asked him what he thought about the boob job and he didn't hesitate. He said, "Hell yeah, go for it!" She broke up with him for that—not because he wanted her to get the makeover, but because he didn't have to think about it longer than two seconds. Of course he got mad and called her a crazy whore. I hate guys who immediately go for the insults that hurt the most. He knew what it was like to work at H------ and how they made waitresses stand at the door and compete for customers like they were prostitutes at the Bunny Ranch. He also knew that during those days before rehab she went with some douchebag guys who posted pictures of her. Every time he called her a whore he tapped into that. I didn't hate Jake because he hurt Anya: I hated him because he could charm his way back every time. Even girls who are pretty smart can be pretty dumb when it comes to guys.

Anya decided to do the makeover and the website's numbers went into the stratosphere. All of a sudden everyone wanted to be a part of remaking our former television star. Javier taped the whole thing (We not only are able to pay him now but even give him a crew—yay! [Pictures of Javier, Dave and Austin (mm10ab)] One major issue was whether or not to show Anya's chest on camera and the procedure of cutting around the nipple. Anya gave us permission because she was tired of hearing about girls still in high school asking for boob jobs for a graduation gift; she wanted them to know what they would be getting into. [Pics of Anya resting after surgery (mm11ab)] I have always looked down on women who opted for implants--if nature gave you small breasts be a big girl and deal with it. I never thought about the recovery from the surgery, but it turns out that it's a bigger bigger deal than I thought. They gave her some Vicodins, but they didn't help much because she puked them back up. Anya was still sore when she went on *The Today Show*. Even though she was pissed about it, she pretended to be happy with the fan's choice during the interview. I used to think that one of the things that sucked about being a kid was the lack of power and always having to do things you didn't want to do, but it's pretty much the same when you're an adult. As long as you want something—whether it's money or security or fame— sometimes you have to do things you don't want to do.

When I was six years old, my mom and I took a train into New York to go shopping on Canal Street and try to get on the *Today Show*. We stood outside on the sidewalk holding a sign that said *WE LUV AL ROKER!* That was back when Roker was a little rounder and didn't have his own show. I can't get used to his face now, (No offense, Al!) but I'm horrible when it comes to change. Back when I was a kid, every time my parents wanted to take down wallpaper or paint a room a new color I would flip out, and I'm like that with people, too. That's why working on a project that involves making over my best friend is a big deal for me.

Anyway, Al didn't fall for it and we didn't get our chance to wave hello to a bunch of people we see every day at home. Yet there I was just twelve years later—associate producer of one of the hottest websites around. It was crazy cool to be on the inside looking out at all those people. I arranged it so that Dr. Huang, who did the surgery, was on the show with Anya—this gave him free publicity and us a free boob job. For the first time I thought I had a knack for that position.

Chapter 5

New Digs

Week Five

It was our turn to pick the category and we all breathed a sigh of relief. We decided that now that Anya was a celebrity again, she needed a bigger place; therefore, the next category was "A New Apartment." We had to include some requirements like price range and square feet, and of course it had to be located in one of the boroughs of the city, but that's about it. The fans found some awesome deals which was a nice reminder of why we did this website in the first place. But once again we had these creepy makeover suggestions—apartments that were in dangerous neighborhoods or ones that looked like drug dens. [Pictures of some mad ugly apartments (mm12abc)] Some jerk even sent us a picture of a dog house in Brooklyn. Thank God that one didn't win.

Even Anya had to admit that there was a fringe population of fans who were seriously trying to sabotage her and the site. The winning apartment was in Soho, which was in the upper end of the price range but otherwise perfect. Snakey Jakey was back in the picture (of course) and he moved in with her. Yesterday *Maury* did a show featuring the more dedicated fans of *makemeover.us*. Some of the people he had on his show were cool but others were borderline psychotic.   Obviously, @mebecraze was there wearing her black wig and showing off the Tree of Life tattoo on her shoulder. I wasn't sure how she was going to keep this up and move into a Soho apartment, but it would be fun to see how far she got. I give her credit for having a goal in life.

Chapter 6

Fixing up the New Digs

Week Six

The category was "Decorating the New Apartment." We uploaded a video of Anya and Jake showing the fans all of their furniture, their pictures, various knick-knacks. Does anyone still use that word? My mom had a lot of crystal figurines and little (empty) chocolate boxes, and it was my job to dust them. When they moved to Florida she asked me to pick the ones I wanted because she was donating the rest to Good Will. I didn't pick any. Really, I wanted all of them, but that was impossible considering that I had to share an apartment that was smaller than my old living room at home, and choosing just one was too hard.

When I was nine, for her birthday I gave my mom this figurine of a girl holding a bunch of dandelions. Maren and I used to call them wishing flowers; once their yellow petals turned into beige mops of hair we'd make a wish and then blow. Of course, now I realize that all we were doing was giving our neighbors more weeds to pull, but back then I thought we were spreading wishes along with flowers. I thought my mom would at least want to keep that one, but she put it in the box marked **Charity** along with the others.

The fans could throw out anything either Anya or Jake owned except photo albums and family mementos. Almost all of Jake's stuff went into the dumpster because his taste consisted of sports posters and beer signs (ha-ha!). One of my favorite fans, SetsbyJoel82, who is an actual set designer, submitted the winning makeover that combined traditional stuff with modern touches in a cool way (370,146 Likes). I've always wanted a claw bathtub—no nouveau riche hot tub for me. [Blurry picture of Joel. He needs to upgrade his cell (mm13a)]

We uploaded videos of Jake and Anya in the bathtub surrounded by candles (cliché or what?!) or hanging some of the artwork Joel picked out. Jake had a meltdown on camera and said he'd never be caught dead sleeping in the four poster bed because it was too girly. He said that he wouldn't sell out to Joel or any other fan and stomped out of the apartment.

Secretly I sort of understood his point on that one because even though it didn't have linen panels or ruffles or anything, if I were a guy it wouldn't be my first choice, but that's the deal with *makemeover.us*. I knew he'd get over it and move back in because like herpes, he never stayed away for very long.

Chapter 7

Jake—Treasure or Trash?

Week Seven

Anya was scheduled to be on the next cover of *Rolling Stone* magazine and we needed something big for her to talk about in the interview, something more dramatic than clothing or hair or interior design. Of course, Jake was already begging Anya to give the relationship another shot. Despite her tough talk last weekend ("This time I'm done." "I deserve better." Blah, blah, blah), I can tell she's wavering, which inspired me to come up with Week Seven's category "Jake: Keep Him or Toss Him to the Curb for Good?" I've been hoping Anya would develop the strength to get rid of that parasite for a while now and using the fans to do my dirty work was underhanded, but you could've knocked me over with a feather when Anya agreed to it.

That's another one of my mother's old-timey expressions. *BTA* I used to tease her about them all the time. My favorite was "a last hurrah." Apparently it means a last big fling. I guess our lives were one last hurrah right up until Gina's birthday bash. That was one of the reasons why my mother resigned from her job—if she couldn't convince her own daughter not to drink and drive, how could she influence anybody else's kid? From what her friends tell me, Maren wasn't even much of a drinker; as an athlete she was super careful about what she put into her body. This is why her friends always made her the designated driver. That night she had maybe two beers, and they were *Lights*. Two of her friends were in the car, one got away with minor injuries, but Heather's spine was permanently damaged, which is why Fairfield is a dead end for me.

The fans LOVED the category and had heated debates about whether Anya should give Jake one more chance or not. He actually posted a video on the fans' YouTube channel pleading his case. He can be deceptively charming, which is why I privately referred to him as Snakey Jakey, except when drunk, in which case I said it to anyone with ears. Normally, I don't like being on camera, but I asked Anya if I could give the fans some background on their relationship. Long story short—I won and Jake lost. The fans remembered his little tantrum about the bed and his snide comments about Joel. Anya needed to make her own decisions, and with Jake out of the picture, everything would be a lot easier. Without Jake and the constant drama that goes with him, Anya could focus on what was important.

Chapter 8

The Fans Take Over

Week Eight

Some categories suggested by the fans: "Plastic Surgery" (again!), "A Blind Date," "A New Acting Coach," "Piercings," and "Scarification."

Of course it was the psychotic fringe who suggested Scarification, which is basically body art through self-mutilation. [Picture of random person with scarification (mm14a)] One time at H------ this customer showed me his scar, which was a bullet wound in his shoulder. He had to hire a guy who was an expert at shooting a person without hurting any organs or causing muscular damage. I guess there is a perfect spot in the shoulder. The guy thought it would turn me on, which is one indication of the intelligence of some of the dudes who go to H------. I watched Anya's face as she read the categories. She pulled back and went inside herself. I don't know what we all thought would happen when we started this, but that was the problem: we didn't think much at all. The next day the fans began voting. I uploaded a video showing exactly what scarification was and telling the fans how important it was for them to remember the original intent of the website. We needed the good fans to stand up against the bad ones and prove that we couldn't let Anya become a voodoo doll to poke at.

The psychotic fringe retaliated by blasting me on Twitter and Tumblr, claiming that I was trying to mess with the nature of the show and take control away from the fans. They tried to spin it into a philosophical stand against oppression, which is insane. One fringe fan said that my comment about voodoo dolls showed that I was a racist. (Really?!) We all think we get it about the downside of being famous—we look at Lindsay Lohan or Amanda Bynes and think we could avoid their fates because somehow we would be smarter and able to stay grounded, but the only way to find out how fame would change you is by becoming a celebrity, and then it's too late.

Anya came from a stable family; her parents tried to enforce rules but it's not easy when your child is surrounded by jerks and is making tons of money. One good thing they did was put most of her money in a trust fund that she could only access when she turned 25. They figured by then she'd be mature enough to spend it. Unlike my parents, they wanted Anya to go to college, but she chose to live in New York City instead and "concentrate on becoming a real actress" like Marilyn Monroe.

We began to notice a few paparazzi hanging around in the street outside the apartment. Anya retreated to her four poster bed and watched reruns of *Bewitched* and *I Dream of Jeannie* on ME-TV. I find it therapeutic to lose myself in a past decade when the clothes and the cars were different, but being an actor Anya likes to take these shows apart and analyze them. She thought it was interesting that both shows are about how many problems are caused by these women having superpowers. Daren and Tony were always yelling at the girls for wiggling a nose or crossing two arms and blinking. I couldn't help wondering—if these sitcoms were made today and if the women were in lesbian relationships, would their partners still try to pressure them into not using their special powers? I would say yes. No one likes to be the side kick, whether it's a girl or a guy.

I made chocolate chip cookies because when I'm nervous I like to eat raw cookie dough, and Javier and his crew were always in the mood for food. [Pictures of Javier eating my amazing cookies (mm15abcd)] It's probably obvious that I had a thing for Javier, but I knew he had a girlfriend. Usually I went for guys who looked older, but he was too cute to resist. When I first met him I even wondered if he was gay because he put out zero sexual vibes. But I guess he's just one of those guys who doesn't see every girl as a piece of meat (Just my luck!). For most of the day and into the night the voting was close, but by 11:30 PM we felt confident in calling it: the winning category was more "Plastic Surgery."

I was relieved but also sick to my stomach, partly from the cookie dough but mostly because Anya would freak. I think the plastic surgery suggestion bothered her almost as much as the scarification; like most girls, she had issues with her body but it's tough when millions of people agree with you. I took a Tylenol PM and slept on Anya's couch; the "good" fans had outnumbered the fringe, but it had been close and I did not want to think about the future. [Picture of me passed out on the couch (mm16a)]

The winning makeover was rhinoplasty which is basically a nose job. If you look at Anya's nose, the bridge does not follow a perfect line, but that's what makes her face interesting. [Close-up of Anya's face (mm16.5)] Beauty is not necessarily about perfection, sometimes it's a flaw that sets off the exquisite. I took an online course in Art Appreciation and that idea seemed perfect to me. I haven't settled on a major but I like picking up random information. When Anya heard about the makeover she went to the bathroom and looked into the mirror for a long time. She told us that everyone in her family said she had her father's nose. She called home from her bedroom and cried as she told her parents about the upcoming surgery.

I think she was worried that the next time she looked in the mirror, between the bigger boobs, the hair, and the new nose, she wouldn't recognize herself. I am almost positive she called Jake too. I'll bet he learned from his last mistake with the boob job and waited a few minutes before telling her to get her nose fixed. Later though, when they had one of their usual fights, he used it against her—called her Barbie and said she sold out. Personally, I was relieved to hear her cry. I know that sounds weird because it's hard to watch someone unravel, but it's even worse to watch someone disappear.

That's what my father did in the ATA period—he retreated inside himself and never came back out. That night in the hospital when the doctors told us the news his face changed into wet cement and then hardened. My dad wasn't an athlete in high school—more of the class editor of the yearbook type—but he has a talent with numbers and knew all the stats of his favorite players, whether it was baseball, football, whatever. When he realized that his oldest daughter not only loved sports but was good at playing basketball and softball, he was beyond thrilled. Losing Maren was losing his best buddy, and there was no way I could make up for that.

For a while, I tried to bone up on sports trivia, but it was no good. I don't have that kind of memory for details, and he didn't want to watch a game on Sundays anymore anyway. Not that he didn't love me, because of course he did. He does. But nowadays when I work up the nerve to visit, we make conversation. We talk about the weather (hot), the humidity (high), and television shows (*Game of Thrones*). Two days are my limit.

If you've ever watched someone get rhinoplasty, it can be pretty brutal. (In Greek rhino means nose but all I can think about is the actual rhino, which is surprisingly cute). The doctor had to break  Anya's nose in order to sculpt it so that it would look good. Watching his big shoulders bent over her made her look so little and helpless. I know she was under general anesthesia so she felt no pain, but Anya believes that our bodies store memories of moments in which they experience trauma. She thinks that if too many violent memories are stored in your cells, it can cause problems down the road.

Seriously. She meditated for a long time before the surgery, telling her body what would happen and trying to soothe it. She's as new age as they get, but who knows? Nobody can explain phantom leg pain but that doesn't mean it doesn't hurt like crazy. My cousin Bryan got back from Afghanistan last year and he had a buddy who lost a leg; it still hurts him in the middle of the night even though it's not technically there.

Yeah, I know what she called me. I used to think it was because I met Anya at a meeting and maybe she thought I'd relapse and drag Anya down with me. I'd been clean for eleven months, didn't drink or smoke weed, which is more than I can say for Rhiannon or that camera crew she hired. Everybody's talking about heroin now. It's all over the news.

What happened to Philip Seymour Hoffman is an addict's worst nightmare, especially since he'd been clean for what, twenty years?

There's always this voice in the back of your head, 'Come back. You can handle it. It'll be okay this time.' I heard he said that at least if he died the media coverage would stop about ten people from overdosing. I don't know. The death penalty never stopped anybody from committing murder because nobody thinks they're gonna get caught.

When it came to Anya, I screwed up. Posted pictures with other girls that I

knew would piss her off. Ignored her texts just to see how bad she'd blow up my phone. We both played games, trying to see who had the upper hand. But if she caught me messing around, I owned up to it and tried to work it out.

I wrote Anya a song once after a fight, but did I put that up on YouTube? No. Some things should be private. Which is a concept Anya didn't buy into. She started this whole makemeover thing without even asking for my opinion.

I'm not saying she had to ask my permission, but considering I was supposed to be a major part of her life, you'd think she'd talk to me about it. I wasn't crazy about being told where I had to live. That apartment they picked was a lot farther from the garage where I park my truck. And she let them throw my stuff into a dumpster. How many guys would put up with that? I don't care who she is.

My theory is that Anya's best friend wants to be a little more than best friends. The whole time I was with Anya, I never saw Rhiannon go out with a guy. Maybe a little making out in a bar when she was drunk, but that's about it. She couldn't wait to get me out of the picture. It started with little sleepovers but it didn't take long before she worked her way into that four poster bed. So you tell me who the real snake is.

Chapter 9

Red Flags

Week Nine

Anya was not herself. For one thing, she wasn't sleeping. At first, her sleep was messed up due to the surgery, but after a while her inner clock got out of whack and she slept about three hours a night and then took naps throughout the day. There are like five stages of sleep everyone is supposed to go through and three hours is not enough time to cycle into REM sleep (Who knew Intro to Psych would come in handy?). She walked around like a zombie—didn't care where we went for lunch, what we watched on TV—and she refused to think up a category.

As associate producer, I decided that we could kill two birds with one stone (Yep, Mom again. I don't know why I was thinking about her so much. I decided that once things calmed down with the website, I would definitely fly to Florida for a visit. At least we'd have something to talk about.

That week's category: "Finding Help for Anya"

The fans debated about the positives and negatives of anti-depressants versus holistic healing like Reiki and Yoga. Dr. Drew's people contacted us about Anya appearing on the show. Luckily, one of the fans was a psychiatrist (Dr. Leander). She made a good case on YouTube and won by a landslide. [Picture of Dr. Leander (mm17a)] The fringe wasn't interested in the category and barely voted. This was a great indication of the diverse range of our audience—we didn't only attract nerds and cross dressers—we appealed to all kinds of demographics. The only problem was that once you go Lexapro you never go back. At least I didn't. Dr. Leander usually only saw her patients about once every two months to check on meds, but because of her personal interest she also acted as Anya's therapist. After Maren's death, my parents put me into therapy and all I can say is that it's exhausting. I stopped going when I turned seventeen because at some point there is nothing else to say. I'm waiting for time to heal all wounds.

Chapter 10
Doctor's Orders

Week Ten

The first thing that Dr. Leander ordered was that Anya take a week off so that she could visit her family and get her sleep groove back. [Pictures of Dr. Leander and Anya (mm17.5abc)]. Because the fans had chosen her, they didn't put up much of a fuss. Anya and I flew into the Charleston South Carolina Airport and her parents picked us up and drove us to Grassy Creek—Anya wanted to rent a car but you have to be at least twenty-one. We can rent an apartment but not a car. Unbelievable! Her mom grew up in this adorable old house right near a marsh and took it over about a year ago when Anya's grandfather had to go into a nursing home. They have a stable with three horses and a pool with a cabana. I felt like I had just stepped into the pages of some gothic southern novel; all this visit needed was a cotillion ball full of debutantes.

The town was so picturesque I almost wished we had brought Javier and the guys, but I'm glad we didn't because it was amazingly cool to spend entire days NOT thinking about what the fans might think of next. We helped her mom in the garden, watched home movies, and checked out Charleston [Pictures of us getting ice cream and little girl asking for Anya's autograph (mm18abc)]. Anya offered to teach me to ride but I was barely on the horse for five minutes when I broke out in hives. (Nope, not putting up a pic of me with hives. I looked hideous.) I spent the rest of the day in Anya's pool drinking *homemade* lemonade. Yum!

Anya slept more and the whole time we both felt free, free, free—right up until the morning we had to board the plane to return to New York. The minute we loaded our bags into the car, I felt this tarp of dread descend over me. When our plane started circling LaGuardia, Anya began to cry. She begged me to move into the apartment when we got back. I hesitated—her couch was fine once in a while, but it hurt my back if I slept on it too often. She offered to share the four poster bed with me; it was a king size so there would be plenty of room for both of us. Some of the other passengers were looking at us and a few took pictures with their cells. I didn't want the psycho fringe spreading rumors about her being even more unstable, so I said yes. But I didn't feel good about it. The closer you get to someone the more it hurts when things go bad.

Chapter 11

Giving Back

Week Eleven

We decided that the project should be less narcissistic; once in a while it needed to focus on something other than Anya, so when she appeared on *Conan* Anya announced this week's category was "Choosing a Public Service Opportunity." Conan had a few of the lunatic fringe on his show and got a lot of laughs from @Frybaby's bizarre theory about Anya's role in the end of days and Mikey21560, who got down on one knee and proposed to Anya on the show. This only made our girl seem more normal which is exactly what every associate producer wants.

One of the fans, RobnSue, called the category choice "a blatant attempt to pander to the public," and I hate to say it but Rob was right. (I've discovered that it's no coincidence that associate producer begins with '*ass.*') That's what it was for me, but for Anya it was different. She was already getting the fame she wanted: she needed to like herself again. The makeovers suggested by the fans ranged from volunteering at a soup kitchen to picking up trash on the highway. The fringe obviously voted heavily for garbage duty because they wanted to do some drive-bys and toss trash at us, but we actually ended up volunteering at a Special Olympics event which was beyond awesome.

Jake turned up to help and I warned Anya that she was playing with fire. If the fans found out they were back together there would be a backlash. (She said that they were only friends and that it was a free country, blah, blah blah) We made sure he wasn't in any footage we used and kept them apart most of the day. The problem was that keeping them apart only made it more certain they would get back together. Luckily Austin is amazing when it comes to editing; if you can watch slo-mo footage of Anya hugging participants after they crossed the finish line and not have tears in your eyes, you're not human. Best photo op ever. We were in Gangnam Style territory. It turned out that I was pretty good at associate producing; maybe I've got my father's head for numbers.

Chapter 12

Paradise Lost

Week Twelve

Monday morning and neither one of us wanted to get up and face the week. It felt as if the bed was a king-size raft and the fans were circling, their fins bobbing up to remind us that it was time to give them a taste. I made us hot chocolate and French toast with lots of syrup, using sugar to handle my nerves once again, but Anya wouldn't eat. She burrowed under the covers and made secret calls to Jake. About two o'clock she showered and said she was going to the gym, but I knew where she was really going. I let her lie to me because what else could I do? She thinks that with her love Jake will mature into a man she can count on. I think hoping a person will change into someone better is just sad. Change only occurs when you don't see it coming—like the way knowledge crashed over Oedipus like a tsunami and forced him to be more humble. [Picture of my final paper at my first on-ground course at LaGuardia Community College (mm19a)] Jake will grow up when some big event matures him, and there is nothing Anya can do to speed up that process. But try telling her that. The only thing she has to say about the Greek tragedies is that they're depressing.

While Anya was with Jake, I checked the website and was relieved when I saw some cool makeovers; one was "Hiring a Vocal Coach." Her mother passed on her southern accent to Anya and I guess it would be a good idea to reduce it. "Finding Anya a New Guy" was another popular one, especially since some rumors of Jake being spotted at the Special Olympics were already spreading around. If every week consisted of harmless, good-intentioned makeovers like these I'd be five pounds lighter. It was looking like the fringe had finally lost interest. The winning category turned out to be "Promoting Anya's Career." Nothing to complain about there. To celebrate, that night I went out with Javier, his girlfriend Donna-Marie (sigh), and Austin, and we got completely wasted.

I am a fun girl to party with as long as I don't do shots or take pills. Once in a while though, I let someone talk me into doing shots and the next thing I know I'm popping a few pills. That's when I get a little out of control. My therapist used to tell me that "my self-destructive behavior was an expression of my resentment." It's hard to resent someone who was only 17 when she made a mistake, someone who liked basketball more than boys, someone who is probably still decomposing underground. But I am somehow able to do it. Apparently, I am angry with Maren because she turned my parents into holograms, changed the story of my childhood, and erased my identity before I could figure out what it was.

After the accident, when I did work up the guts to go into town, nobody saw me: they saw the younger sister of the girl who drove drunk and crippled her best friend. My therapist said that having "discovered the cause of my anger, I needed to forgive her." (Therapists are never ever satisfied.) Which sounded good, but I couldn't let it go. I hated Maren more than I loved myself, I guess.

Getting back to that night, for some reason, I was bent on getting annihilated; maybe deep down I knew that the fringe was about to make a move, or maybe I just needed to let loose some of that anger I keep for special occasions. I hardly ever have a problem getting drinks in a club, especially since the place where they ID you is usually dark, but I tend to wear a low-cut shirt just in case. That's pretty much all it takes unless the bouncer is a girl. Even then, sometimes it works on her too. After a bunch of shots of Ciroc Berry Vodka (my fave), I came up with the brilliant idea of altering my tattoo. I started asking guys to carve a knife in Goofy's gloved hand. Actually, I didn't need anybody's help fixing my tattoo because it's located on my right calf, but unlike a lot of girls I know, I can't seem to cut myself. I've tried. Blood freaks me out.

According to Donna-Marie, that night I found some dude who worked as a cook at Dawson's willing to do it. He said he had his own set of knives in the car. To most sane people, following a guy out to his car because he has his own knives is not a smart idea. [Picture of Edward Scissorhands if we can get permission (mm20a)] But when I'm that high I am definitely not smart. Thank God Austin stopped me from leaving the club. He said that if I wanted to give Goofy a knife, I could do it when I was sober at a legit tattoo place with sterile needles. I will probably not do that though because I don't want to deface poor innocent Goofy with his crazy big feet and lovable smile. He can't help stepping on other people's toes once in a while.

The next day, with a hangover the size of Alaska, I saw the winning category and that's when everything went to hell. The fringe hadn't moved on to another target—they had been biding their time. They put up a makeover that started gaining almost immediately. If it were chosen, I couldn't see how we'd be able to continue with the website. There is no way Anya would agree to it and even if she did, I wouldn't let her. At least, I hoped I wouldn't. Uploading a clip on YouTube arguing against it would only empower the fringe. We had to trust that our true fans wouldn't let a makeover like that win out. But Anya was no longer an underdog; she had not only gotten her former fame back but was fast becoming a cult icon; even some of her more loyal fans might like to see her brought down a few pegs.

If Kim Could Do it...

The fringe won. The winning makeover was "Making a Sex Tape." Twitter went apocalyptic and on Reddit fans created a few subreddits either trashing Anya or defending her. (Some of the bloggers on the negative subreddits were way beyond scary. We're talking suggesting things like actual gang rape as part of the sex tape. What is wrong with people?!) All over the internet, the loyal fans ripped into the fringe and the fringe stood their ground. It was a sex tape that launched Kim Kardashian, so why not Anya? They weren't fooling anyone though. Our good fans nailed them for creating a campaign to humiliate Anya. Unfortunately, all this back and forth did no good; we were stuck with the rules we had created. The fans had voted and now we had a decision to make—end the show or make a tape.

Javier, Anya, Austin, and I got together in her living room to talk about how to respond to the makeover. Anya is no prude and as an actress she has always been prepared for the idea that she might have to do a nude scene—but a sex tape is a different beast. Kim Kardashian might be famous, but she would never be taken seriously as a performer. On the other hand, if we closed down the site, this would mean that the fringe had won. Anya was very quiet. She was waiting for us to say don't do the tape, but none of us said that. She looked at me and I said, "We'll do whatever you want. You're the boss." She looked down at her hands and a little smile played over her mouth, but it was one of those expressions people make when their worst fears are confirmed. She looked directly at me and said, "You're just like everybody else" and then grabbed her purse and walked out of the apartment.

Looking back, I probably shouldn't have put her in the spot of having to decide between her pride and the site. Yes, it was ultimately her decision, but she needed a friend to stand by her. Instead she had an associate producer who was only thinking about the project. Too many of us were now depending on it for our existence. All of us sitting around that coffee table were making real money for the first time in our lives, and we were part of a phenomenon. No one wanted the ride to end except maybe Anya.

I tried to text her but her cell was off. Even Jake said he didn't know where she was, but that was a lie. The clock was ticking. We had to make our decision about whether to do the makeover or not by midnight. It was Javier who came up with the solution—we would make a parody of a sex tape instead— make it deliberately zany—*A Hard Day's Night* meets *World Wide Wrestling*. It had to be so bad it was good; if the fans decided it was lame (like the one the Spice Girls did) we'd lose them anyway.

Jake brought Anya back to the apartment at about 10 PM that night. When we told her our plan, she wasn't that impressed. She didn't want to be the butt of a joke, especially if it involved her naked butt. I told her that if WE made the joke, we could control the laughter. If we clearly didn't take it seriously, then the media wouldn't either. Think *The Scary Movies, Blazing Saddles, Austin Powers,* YouTube's *The Key of Awesome,* all those skits by Keenan and Peele. Parodies are targeted at people with a twisted sense of humor and it's kind of a compliment if you get the joke. We could hire a couple of professional writers to help out so that the jokes wouldn't be too cheesy.

Eventually she agreed—she would make the tape as long as I appeared in it with her. (Grrrh!) She knew how I felt about being on camera, especially if it involved having hardly any clothes on, so I fought her on this. What surprised me was that Jake backed me up. He definitely didn't think it was a good idea for me to play a part in the scene. I'm not sure if he was trying to do me a favor or what, but neither one of us got our way. If Anya wanted me in, I was in. She was the star and she knew it.

A few of the former writers from SNL used to come in to H------ once in a while, so I hired two of them for an all-night brainstorming session. I went to one of those sex stores and bought a whole bunch of stuff—a sexy police officer's costume including the hat, the gloves and the mirror sunglasses (all with rhinestones), a dog color and a leash, a blow-up doll named Veronique, some furry handcuffs. You would not believe some of the crazy things they had in there!

They had this blow-up doll of Obama with some kind of slogan about his *stimulus package* that I thought was really rude. Like him or don't like him, but it seemed to me that the president of our country shouldn't be on that kind of merchandise.

I told the SNL guys to make up a story with the props. I have to admit that it was kind of fun to be the one giving them money for a change. God I loved being in charge. They had Anya playing a lonely woman in a hotel room on a business trip. She orders a pizza, hoping to get lucky with the pizza delivery dude. The pizza dude arrives but inside his box is a bunch of sex toys instead of a pizza. Things get loud, some customers in nearby hotel rooms hear the noise and ask to join the party, a cop is called (played by me), somebody pulls a fire alarm, and we all run out of the hotel wearing each other's clothes (Super corny, I know!). The sex would all be faked— and it would look faked.

Anya wanted to give Jake the Pizza Dude role but I said no. The fans had voted him out of Anya's life; it was important right now to show that we were following the rules, especially since we were bending them by creating this parody. If the fans felt that we weren't at least holding up our end, they'd disappear and there would be no getting them back. I said we should have Austin do it because Javier and Dave have to operate the camera and sound equipment. Anya said that if I didn't like Jake as the Pizza Delivery Dude, I could leave.

It was the second time she had gone against me, and it cut deep. No one could deny that the only reason I had this job was because Anya wanted me there. If she no longer did, what right did I have to stay? During the last few months I had made deals, hired lawyers to sort out the financial issues, consulted social media experts, even took on a few interns—I was good at this job. But there was no way I could do it if Anya undermined my authority, so I offered to quit. I looked at the guys hoping they would back me up. Austin agreed to be in the film (I'm pretty sure he was dying to show off his abs), and Javier said that the last thing we needed was to piss off the fans. Anya caved but told me that she would rather I slept in my own apartment from now on.

The video was a humungous hit because it showed that Anya had a sense of humor. [Pictures after filming the sex tape (**mm21ab**)] E! and Tosh were all over it. [Anya got into the dominatrix role, I guess (**mm21cd**)] and one more [Pillow Fight! (**mm21ef**)]. We sent Perez Hilton some special footage with funny bloopers and he featured a clip on Perez TV. Anya had a soft spot for Perez because I guess back in her drug days he could've posted this embarrassing clip of her but he didn't, so she wanted to be sure that he got some exclusive footage. I voted for Anya to appear on either *The Colbert Report* (to get that Colbert bump!) or *Late Night with Jimmy Fallon* (that was before he got the *Tonight Show*) because I really wanted to meet Jimmy; he's the kind of guy you wish you had for an uncle because he'd make every Thanksgiving dinner funny and cool.

Since my parents moved to Florida, we've given up celebrating Thanksgiving, so at least I don't have to worry about my father trying to make up things we should be grateful for. Some of the more extreme members of the fringe were mad, but the smarter nutjobs conceded that we had outmaneuvered them. I only hoped our loyal fans got the point—vote or lose control of the site. There is actually a group of fans who want me to have my own makeover channel, but I am way not into that. It's hard enough just being the producer of this chaos. (Yep, I gave myself a promotion.) That night I had this dream that I was walking on a tightrope and the net below kept getting smaller every time I looked down. I guess promotions come with a price.

Chapter 13

Six Feet Underwater

Week Thirteen

Mr. Allen (Anya's dad) called with news that her Aunt Rosalyn died. It would be easier to list what organs DIDN'T have cancer. Very sad. According to the will, she wanted her ashes sprinkled in the ocean off Cape Cod, so the family was renting a yacht and having a service on the sea. I don't like funerals and I am not a fan of long car trips (give me a plane or train any day), but I offered to go with Anya to the Cape and attend the funeral. I wanted to do something to fix things between us. She agreed—I guess she is better at forgiveness than I am.

I also offered to close down the site for a week so that Anya could concentrate on her family; I knew this was a bad idea but I needed to show her that she was my first priority. I was counting on the fact that the site meant as much to her as it did to me; one week without activity could lose millions of fans. Anya said no, we could find a way to combine the makeover with the trip to the Cape. (Phew!) But the really important thing was that she and I were friends again.

We put up this week's category: "Saying Something Memorable."

Mr. Allen was giving the eulogy, but he asked Anya to say something about her aunt as well. Of course, Anya had a few stories about Aunt Roselyn ready to go, but adding a quote or philosophical observation would be a nice way to include the fans. We released a video of Anya talking about her aunt and showing clips of home movies featuring Rosalyn. [Pic of Aunt Rosalyn (mm22a)] We gave info on donating to a cancer research center and offered to match any fan's contribution. Anya also told the fans that this was no time for pranks. Only appropriate comments should get votes. It was time for the true fans to take back the site!

We got some terrific makeover quotes which made us feel good about people again. At least some people. My favorite was from *Fight Club*: "I don't want to die without any scars." That's what Anya didn't have before *makemeover.us*. Scars. Not the real kind. Sure she struggled when the series got cancelled, but she always knew she had her trust fund to fall back on. She slummed it at H------ for a few months, but only because she wanted to *experience real life*. As the fans pulled her strings and made her dance, she was getting marked up by life a little.

I also thought the quote by William Burroughs was interesting, though obviously not appropriate for Anya's Aunt Rosalyn. He said that "Nobody owns life, but anyone who can pick up a frying pan can own death." Cool, right? Murder is the ultimate power play that most of us never use. But we all know it's an option.

Of course, the fringe put up some stupid quotes, but this time each of them didn't get more than 50 or so Likes. Maybe death is one thing that people still respect. I couldn't tell you what was said at the service (aside from the makeover tip we chose) because I didn't listen to a word of it. I really cannot take funerals, even when they concern people I don't know. I took an extra Lexapro and hummed "Let it Be" in my head the whole time. @mebecraze sent this big wreath with white and red carnations—the kind that stands on an easel. We put it next to the collage of pictures from Aunt Rosalyn's life. I may be crazy but she was definitely becoming my fave tranny. [Picture uploaded by @mebecraze of her picking out the wreath (mm23.5ab)]

Coming up with categories had become a real bitch. (Out of respect for my mom, I generally try not to swear, but most people don't even consider this a swear because it's also the name of a female dog, and even for those who do, it's one of the minor league ones, so I'm keeping it in.) We had to choose something that the normal fans would find fun but the fringe couldn't pervert into something embarrassing. Luckily, this category practically fell in our laps.

After we sprinkled the ashes at sea, Anya checked her iPhone and saw a bunch of stupid pictures on Jake's Facebook and Instagram. I guess while we were in the Cape, Jake was partying it up with some girl named Zoe who probably had about half a dozen STDs. [Pictures of Jake with STD Girl hanging all over him (mm24abc)] Anya felt really betrayed because she thought Jake's friends liked her, but they were the ones who partied with him that night and took a lot of those pictures. Plus, Anya wasn't happy about some of his new followers and the tweets they were sending back and forth. I didn't bother to say, "We'll, you guys ARE broken up" because we both knew that they weren't truly broken up for good. I've been on this ride with Anya a dozen times and she always ends up going back, but for Anya each time it happens, it's a shock.

> Stage 1: *Anger*. She tweets that she is so over him and rants about what a jerk he is. She calls friends she hasn't seen in a while, goes out to clubs and makes out with random guys.

> Stage 2: *Complete melt-down*. This stage consists of crying and/or yelling into a cell phone.

> Stage 3: *Numbness*, marked by blank stares and despair. Communication blackout. This stage bothers me the most.

> Stage 4: *Back peddling*. She communicates with Jake and he tells her how much he misses/loves her. She starts saying that the fight either really was HER fault or that she over-reacted depending on the cause of the fight. He writes her a poem or brings her a flower or pulls some other manipulative crap.

> Stage 5: *Together again*. They are blissfully happy for about 4 to 6 days and have learned to appreciate one another. Then back to Stage 1.

Chapter 14
Anya the Bachelorette

Week Fourteen

We announced the category: "A Date for Anya" and gave the fans 24 hrs. to upload videos of men who were interested in going out on a date. Having learned from our experiences with the fringe, we also released a few requirements:

- Candidates had to be heterosexual males (aside from some bi-curious moments, Anya was basically straight)
- Not in a relationship (of course)
- They had to be between the ages of 19-30 (she likes older men)
- They could not have a police record (aside from minor traffic violations)
- They had to be human (no animals, no blow up dolls, etc.)
- They had to be employed (we didn't want guys looking for a meal ticket)
- They had to live in the tri-state area (no long distance relationships, thank you)

- Each video could only contain one candidate (no three-ways!)

All candidates would be screened and any dude who didn't meet the requirements would be tossed out. For this category I had some serious work to do: I had to hire more staff to vet the candidates and find a location for the date that worked for Javier and that also appealed to Anya. Despite her concerns, I also decided to hire security; lots of people recognized her, and I couldn't take a chance that one of the psycho fringe didn't follow her around. I told Anya it's different when you hire them versus your parents because you can fire them anytime you want and they know that. I hoped that the category would not only be popular with the fans but might also actually stop the stupid cycle of pain she and Jake were in (fingers crossed!).

Anya tweeted about some of the guys and commented on their videos. She can really flirt when she wants to. Jake freaked out, which was her intention, I'm sure. She wanted to go out clubbing that night (of course) but I put my foot down and said no—I didn't want some video coming up on E! of her drunk dancing and hanging all over some guy. When a girl wants to get back at a guy, that's a "special occasion" in Anya's book. (Reality check: If you're decent looking, the bracelets they give you in clubs that tell bartenders whether they can serve you or not are meaningless. Guys either buy you drinks or the bartenders do hoping you'll be *nice* to them later. And if you're famous and pretty, regardless of your age, there is no bracelet.)

We didn't want the cops trolling the internet looking for evidence to arrest Anya for violating her probation. Dr. Leander backed me up on this (Anya saw her twice a week). Nevertheless, Anya was pissed off because she was used to appeasing her anger with attention from other men, but I made us a big bowl of popcorn and we watched the uploaded YouTube videos of hundreds of guys who wanted to be Anya's next boyfriend. That should've been enough male attention, even for a former television star.

Some of them were definite Nos, but others were cute (Simon, Liam, Antonio—top three) or funny (Tim!), muscle-bound (Jorge!) and a few had really good jobs (Financial Broker, Physician's Assistant, Chiropractor). Of course, lots of actors uploaded what can only be called auditions with monologues. Both of us hoped that the fans wouldn't choose one of those. Anya needed a boyfriend, not a competitor. [Pictures of the top contestants (mm24.5abcd)]

I had my interns gather tons of pictures of cute restaurants that had private rooms. (Because I'm only eighteen and homeschooled, and they have been through some major colleges—one is even from an Ivy—I really love being able to say "my interns.") We wanted something out of the city (parking—ugh!) and yet not too far out of the way. Eventually, Anya and I chose this restaurant that has a very sweet terrace with a fountain in the back that we could rent out for the date. [Picture of private terrace in back of Grazilia's Garden (mm25a)] Javier scouted the location and took two security guards with him. I went out and bought four headsets and walkie-talkies—it felt very CIA.

The winning makeover was.....Rayhan from Darien, Connecticut. He was an engineer at Cisco, 26 years old, originally from Simsbury, recent MIT grad, liked watching and playing sports, going to museums, and hanging out with friends. Anya was not unhappy with the fans' makeover choice because if there was one thing Jake wouldn't do is walk around a museum with her. [Pictures of Rayhan (mm26ab)] Just his name, Rayhan, wraps around you like a silk scarf. I had an intern make sure that he really did work at Cisco, was a citizen, was NOT in a relationship, and didn't have a record. From what we could tell, he seemed legit. Jake would go ballistic. (ha-ha!) Of course, a group of the psycho fans posted some crazy comments as soon as he won—one said we should search him in case he had a string of bombs taped around his waist. There are a lot of angry people out there. Everybody still blames 911, but c'mon. You'd think our country would've gotten past race hatred by now, but the only thing that changes are the targets, which is why the psycho fans can suck it because Rayhan won and he's hot.

Just for fun we allowed the fans to pick Anya's outfit. To avoid unnecessary headaches from the fringe, we limited the choices to particular store website or pics from Anya's closet (lots of retail therapy excursions over the last two months) and told them to choose from those two sources. Fans used their apps to upload Anya in various combinations of outfits which was also a nice distraction for Anya who tended to disappear into her room sometimes to cry over Jake's Twitter feed. Nevertheless, she was not as emotionally wrecked as in past break-ups, so that was a good sign. This was a definite improvement because for once she was showing off that great butt of hers rather than hiding it in some baggy jumper. [Pictures of Anya in the winning dress (mm27abcd)]

I would like to take a break here to discuss why I love vodka. Yes, I realize that I am not legally allowed to consume alcohol here in the U.S., but I go by the European model in which they allow kids to drink to reduce the taboo factor and let them discover their tolerances. I won't even get into the argument about if you can go to war, blah blah blah. Everyone knows that one. Just look at Maren—she hardly ever drank and got killed in a drinking and driving accident. If she had been allowed to legally consume alcohol earlier, say in her freshman year, she would have built up a tolerance so that her coordination wouldn't have been impaired by two **LIGHT** beers. My strategy is A) don't learn to drive and B) always make friends with someone who is willing to be a designated. This way I will never be responsible for the death or life changing injury of another person.

Anyway, back to why vodka is my drink of choice. The biggest reason is that you don't have to taste it unless you WANT to taste it. You could add it to Fruit Punch Gatorade and all you would taste is Fruit Punch Gatorade. Whether you get the expensive kind (Ciroc or Grey Goose) or the cheap kind (Popov, Eeek!) you'll like the drink if you like the mixer. Period. I try to stay away from all brown liquors because whatever you mix them with, you still taste it. (I'm pretty sure Mothers Against Drunk Driving will probably hate me for this, but remember I don't drive. So the only thing I'm putting in danger is my own liver.)

The Not So Blind Date

On a scale of one to ten, it was a disaster. I think most people would say that a first date should not include the police and the ER. We arrived at Grazilia's Garden Terrace at 5:30 pm to set up cameras and talk to the owner. Anya got her hair and make-up done (We now have a make-up person!), the interns had the waiter and owner sign photo releases, and Jav and his crew set up the lights and cameras. Tom and Joe scoped out the place and then hung out in the kitchen eating garlic knots. AT 6:30 PM Tom stood about 200 feet away on the west side of the backyard terrace and Joe was on the east. The terrace had a short 3ft wooden fence with roses twined through it, a trellis also decorated with roses and vines (probably for weddings) and little stone paths. At 6:45 PM Rayhan arrived; our audio guy, Dave, put a mic on him, and he finally met Anya.

They made small talk and ordered drinks; he got an iced tea and she ordered a raspberry lemonade. Apparently he doesn't drink, which would be a bad sign for me because I would wonder if he knew how to have fun, but Anya preferred it given her time in rehab. (When I've gone out with Anya and Snakey Jakey, I couldn't help but notice that he orders a Coke with a lime in it so people don't know he's not drinking, which is so lame—if you're going to give up drinking, then go all in.) Everything was going fine until, speak of the devil, out of the corner of my eye I saw Jake, dressed as a waiter and carrying a basket of bread, walk onto the terrace. I had a split second to decide what to do. We hadn't released the location or name of the restaurant on the site because we didn't want to deal with potentially hundreds of fans, so how did he know where to find us? My guess was that Anya had told him hoping he would come and make a scene. That's why I hesitated to use my new headset and alert Tom and Joe. If Anya wanted him to make a scene, maybe she should have her way; after all, it was her website.

Looking back, I can see that maybe other intentions made me hold off. Maybe I wanted the date to be an epic fail so that I could grab Rayhan for myself. Or maybe I knew that a jealous ex-boyfriend would make great video for the site. Either way, Jake on the scene was a win-win for me. What I didn't see until it was almost too late was the psycho hidden behind the trellis who brought a hot branding iron with him.

Jake threw the basket of bread on the table and started yelling at Anya. You can tell from Rayhan's uploaded video that he is kind of reserved; he's got real style and is not the kind of man who looks for drama. [Pic of Rayhan in case anyone has forgotten how gorgeous he is (mm28a)] I think he was taking a big risk just allowing himself to be on camera, never mind on camera in the midst of a Jerry Springer-like blow-out. Joe and Tommy came rushing in to try to restrain Jake. Anya stood up just as Jake sprang backward to avoid Joe's grasp and (I'm pretty sure) accidentally backhanded Anya right in her new nose. Because the nose was still healing, I think it bled twice as much, but I'm no expert. Noses do bleed a lot. Like head wounds. There is an amazing amount of blood between the brain and the skull. I hadn't taken Human Bio because, as I said, blood grosses me out. Tommy tried to punch Jake, missed and hit the REAL waiter who was walking in to deliver their drinks. Raspberry lemonade and iced tea flew, glasses shattered, and the waiter fell to the floor. Into all of this chaos crept our creep with his branding iron; he was headed towards Anya who was sitting on the ground covering her nose with bloody fingers. Joe and Tom were so busy throwing punches and wrestling Jake that they didn't see him. Rayhan ripped off his mic and took off. I guess Rayhan is a lover, not a fighter.

I grabbed a bottle of Ty Nant, which is this water I started to specially order once we were in the money. I hate drinking water, but I was trying to be more healthy (since then I have given up all healthy habits that I do not enjoy). Ty Nant comes in a pretty cobalt blue glass bottle. It sounds dumb but holding a glass bottle (versus plastic) feels good, especially in hot weather, which made me more apt to drink it. [Picture of me with my Ty Nant water bottle (mm29a)] Anyway, I had a bottle with me on a nearby table, so I grabbed it and hit the psycho fan over the head. He must have felt me behind him because he turned around just as the bottle met his head.

I will never forget the look of surprise that flashed over his face. He lunged toward me with the brand. I jumped to the side but the iron grazed my right arm and I screamed. I don't recall feeling any pain right then, but I do remember the smell of burning flesh. Psycho dude dropped the branding iron and put his hand to his head, which was bleeding like crazy, and Tommy blasted him with his Taser gun. His body jerked and twisted and blood flew from his forehead like sweat—it looked like he was doing some kind of wild dance.

Our psycho had a converter in his car that transformed the power from his lighter into enough volts (120) to heat up an electric iron and brand Anya with his initials **W.S.M**. **[No pic of the branding iron—they had to take it for evidence].** The restaurant's owner called 911 and Anya, the waiter, and I were taken to the hospital while William Stanton Mitchell was handcuffed and arrested. [Pic of Mug shot of William Stanton Mitchell (mm30.5a)] It turned out that Anya did not give Jake the information about the restaurant—our intern Paulina did. The bigger question is how Mitchell obtained the information as well. We needed to hire some IT guys because I had a feeling we were being hacked.

The late nights had fun with the video because we looked like a modern version of *The Three Stooges*. *Good Morning America* wanted both me and Anya to do an appearance but I said no—Anya needed a rest and I didn't want her thinking that I was trying to steal her spotlight. The fan numbers climbed higher and the next day I got calls from HBO and MTV. HBO had a series starting next spring tentatively titled *Steel Drums* and the producers (Rims Productions) were interested in auditioning her for the part of the drummer's girlfriend.

I ended up with half a **W** on my arm, which looks like a **V.** [Picture of my branding scar (mm31ab))] Depending on my mood, I tell people the **V** stands for V*engeance,* V*oila,* V*room!* or V*eronica* (when I don't feel like being me). But no matter what mood I'm in, I never say V*ampire.* (I am totally over vampires and zombies.) Back then I had been a New Yorker for about five months, so I pretended the attack didn't bother me too much: we all knew there are tons of sickos out there. But this guy had meant that branding iron for Anya and no one else. He wasn't out to hurt just anyone, he was out to hurt her. (Or as he would later say in court, "claim" her.) But instead he branded me. I don't usually tell anyone this but for me the real meaning behind the V on my arm is *Vacant.* In my "American Lit: The Ex-Patriots" class, the teacher posted a quote from Gertrude Stein and asked us to say what we thought it meant. The quote was, *"There is no there there."* I put down one word. *"Me."* That's what's great about online education—you never have to see the people you're learning with, so you can say practically anything.

Anya was traumatized, first by Jake's meltdown and then by the attack. She randomly cried off and on all day, which clogged up her nose, making it harder for her to breathe. She even talked about ending the project. I asked Dr. Leander if we should up her meds because Anya was showing signs of deep anxiety. I wasn't sure what her nose would look like once the bandages were taken off, but she absolutely refused to get another nose job. (On the positive side, when it did finally heal, she had Mr. Allen's nose again.) Later the next day, after the higher dosage of meds kicked in, I talked her down from the ledge and mentioned the series targeted for HBO. The big question was whether Rims would still be interested in Anya next spring if we closed the site down now. Maybe they would remember all those times she walked off sets back in the day. She needed to show Hollywood that she was different, that she could stick it out when a production got tough. If she quit now, *makemeover.us* would be just another tabloid headline. I also wasn't shy about pointing out that I had literally saved her skin and deserved some say when it came to wrapping up the project. She agreed to stay on.

I knew we had to give Anya another week off, but we also couldn't risk losing the fans. Jav and I decided that I would fill in for Anya and allow the fans to make me over. Wow! It's one thing to be next to someone doing it, it's another to be the one actually putting yourself under other people's control. Sort of reminds me of the military, although obviously in the military the stakes are much higher, but every soldier has to put his life in the hands of some dude who would make a decision about patrolling an area or taking control of some town square. Military guys can't question anything or go in a different direction, even if all of their instincts tell them to. That's why they have to break them down in boot camp before they build them back up. My Aunt Jody says that my cousin Bryan, the one who did two tours in Afghanistan, is having a hard time finding a job and getting health care. It must be terrible to live in a country that talks about the pursuit of happiness and all that when you can't find a job with benefits. It occurred to me that I could give him a job. (yes, homeschooled ME!) He could whip Joe and Tommy into shape. Because Anya was going to need professional full-time security. One thing we learned from William Stanton Mitchell is that a rising icon needs someone next to her who can fire a gun.

Chapter 15
Subbing for Anya

Week Fifteen

The category was "Make Me Hotter." We changed the rules a little because I was only a substitute for Anya—if I didn't want to do a makeover it shouldn't end the project. But there needed to be some penalty that would be equally epic, so we decided that if I didn't do the makeover, I would have to quit my job as producer of the site. We also decided that my subbing wouldn't be counted as an official week—fans' choice is every fourth week, but that's only when Anya is the one being made over. We announced the new rules on the site and the fans' YouTube channel; of course the fringe gave us a hassle, but most of the normal fans seemed to go for it. They had 24 hrs. to suggest makeovers and Anya got a kick out of watching me get more anxious as the tips rolled in. I guess there are many things one could do to make me hotter: images of tattoos (yawn!), plastic surgery, scarification, hair style changes, clothing options and make-up suggestions poured in. One makeover had me going to rehab for my underage alcohol use. Seriously?! If we put every teenager who drank once in a while into rehab, we'd have to close down the high schools.

The winning entry was enrolling me in "The Couch to 5K" running plan which involves turning me from a couch potato into a jogging potato. Along with the jogging schedule, I had to follow a horrible low carb diet plan. Every day I had to upload videos of me following the plan and filling out a journal on what I'd eaten. I hate thinking about food, never mind keeping track of it. I also despise exercise and love sugar, so this would be two months of torture. [Picture of me making my fave dessert—a banana split (mm32abc)] I will not deny that I had gained a few pounds since this project began and wouldn't mind fitting into some of the clothes cowering in the back of my closet; the deal was that if I didn't lose ten pounds and run a 5K in two months, I would lose my job.

My Stats

Height:	5'6 "
Weight:	141 lbs.
BMI:	22.8

It could've been worse—one fringe member uploaded a makeover that involved lip augmentation [Picture of me posing with fish lips (mm33a)] and another had me growing dreads. I would like to point out that according to many websites, my weight and BMI fall into the "normal" rather than "overweight" category. Only in our society is "normal" not good enough. Being both lazy and impatient, I wouldn't have minded lipo, but the fans want what the fans want, and they wanted me to get skinny the hard way. Bryan offered to train me but after ten minutes I gave up; I have no upper body strength and cannot do a push-up to save my life. But I could alternate walking and jogging as the couch potato program dictates, eat tuna sandwiches minus the sandwich, and cut back on the partying which always results in a carb run.

Anya asked me if I could please stop hating Jake and I said I would try. Mostly I said this because I didn't want him suing the show for damages due to his head injury. I wouldn't have been surprised if he put a claim in for PTSD. If he ever does this I will send Bryan over so that Jake can understand what it means to fear for your life. I guess one thing I needed to figure out was where all this anger towards Jake comes from. Sure, I didn't like the shabby way he treated Anya, but looking back over the last few months I had nothing to brag about. The truth is, I am no different from Jake. Maybe that's why I couldn't stand to look at him.

Chapter 16
Petland

Week Sixteen

We were all in a funk. The core group of us were pretty sick of the routine by now. We were tired of trying to outmaneuver the fringe and frustrated with having to come up with new categories. I was only a few days into my new diet and exercise plan, and I was already wondering whether quitting *makemeover.us* would be such a bad thing. We decided that one way to liven up our lives would be to have a pet— some cute little sweetie that would cheer us all up! So, the next category was "Choosing a Pet". The makeovers went up immediately—adorable pictures of all types of dogs and cats were uploaded, various birds, exotic fish, hamsters, a hedgehog, a rabbit, even an iguana. Naturally the fringe put up their own pics—a snake, a mongoose, a bat, and a Frankenkitty which is a cat that has been bred with wild feral cats. They cost a ridiculous amount of money -- $35,000 can you believe it? Everyone talks about how irresponsible teenagers are but these people are grown adults.

I was hoping for a rabbit because when I was younger I wanted one but my father put his foot down after our hamster (Twix) broke out of his cage and escaped into the furnace ducts, making the house smell like rotting meat for days. Anya wanted to have one of those dogs that fit into a shoulder bag. Bryan wanted the fans to choose a Pit bull; he had two of his own and claimed that they were a very misunderstood breed.

The winning makeover was…a Ball Python. Yep! The fans somehow learned about my nickname for Jake and decided that it would be too funny if we got a snake for our pet. We Googled and found out that a Ball Python is a "docile" species and got its name because it curls up into a ball when frightened. So it is essentially the scaredy-cat of snakes. Why anyone would want a slimy pet when there are plenty of animals that are both furry and cuddly I cannot imagine. The fans REALLY let us down with this one.

Bryan was psyched because, like a lot of army dudes, he gets a kick out of owning animals that could be dangerous. Javier wanted one of those miniature pigs and Austin had his mind set on a hedgehog; actually, Dave kind of looks like a hedgehog. [Pics of Dave and a hedgehog (mm33.5ab)]. We had to wait about two weeks before we could feed it (pythons need to get used to their new homes first or they get stressed out) and the guys were already arguing about who gets to feed it first and whether they should give it a live mouse or a dead one. All morning I heard nothing but various ways to kill a mouse versus a hamster versus a rat. The boys went out and bought the snake and the cage (really an aquarium) with a hideaway room (according to Google, snakes need their alone time). We had to name it Jake as required by the makeover. [Picture of Jake The Python out of his cage (mm34ab)] All in all, a pretty disappointing week. Anya and I talked about buying our own dog, but I think it would be pretty freaked out to have to share an apartment with a Python—even a shy one. I will wait to buy a rabbit when I have my own house in Jersey with a backyard that is big enough to have a cage with multiple levels for burrowing.

Chapter 17
Fandom Rules

Week Seventeen

Anya and I decided to go to the beach—no sense hanging around the apartment checking the website. Plus, I was now down to 138 ½ lbs.—probably just water weight, but it felt good. Bryan, Tommy, and Joe came with us (for security) but Austin and Javier stayed back to "get footage" of the snake. I kept telling them that they had to wait another week to play with the snake or it could get an anxiety disorder and not eat, but I would bet a hundred bucks they couldn't resist taking it out and letting it wrap around their necks. At fairs, when I see guys walking around with snakes wrapped around their shoulders or arms, I think they deserve to get squeezed to death for being stupid.

We've gotten used to the four or five paparazzi who seem permanently stationed outside the front of our apartment building, and the skinny dude who sometimes went dumpster diving in the back ally looking for I don't know what, but another group of fans and paparazzi turned up at the beach. I was glad we had taken our 'security detail' with us—Anya signed a few autographs, posed for a few pictures and then we found a spot near some rocks that Bryan thought would work. We brought three umbrellas (due to my mix of Swedish, Norwegian and English blood, I tend to burn, peel and then burn again) so the guys placed them in such a way that we had some privacy. Bryan made up a schedule and each one of them took turns "on watch." When she was younger, Anya had put up with this stuff for years before the public lost interest in her, but I wonder if anyone ever gets used to being on display yet hidden at the same time.

When it was his turn to take a break and cool off, Bryan thrashed around like a puppy, always moving, either jumping over waves or diving into them. Anya and I tried to hang out on an inner tube but he kept dumping us over, just like the older brother we never had. When Bryan gets out of the water, he whips his hair around and then tips his head to one side and bangs his ear trying to get the water to come out the other side. It looks like something you'd see in a cartoon. I wish he was always this carefree. Aunt Jody called me that morning and said that last night Bryan had had nightmares and was up for hours checking the locks on the doors and windows and walking around the neighborhood. He usually looks like he's dragging a couple of ghosts around with him, but I kind of thought that the waves crashing on his head made him forget his demons, at least for a little while.

This reminds me of that Neitzsche saying everybody including Kelly Clarkson loves—what doesn't kill you makes you stronger. What a bunch of bull. Bryan survived Afghanistan but he is not stronger; my parents survived the death of their daughter but they are not stronger. I think what doesn't kill you can still hurt so much you wish you were dead.

I couldn't help it and checked my iPhone. Some top makeovers were a Sweat Lodge, Yoga Retreat, Drugs (natural and man-made), Reiki, Psychic Reading, Sleep Deprivation (gotta be a fringe choice), and Fasting. Given what she said on the video about being clean from drugs, the makeovers that included drug use struck me as especially mean; it's like they wanted to see her slide back into being a "spoiled diva" so they could make fun of her. Javier put up an announcement warning that Anya could not be required to do anything illegal; fans argued on their YouTube channel that A) the rules never mentioned legality and B) Anya could fly to some place where the particular drug of choice was legal.

Into this perfect day of warm sun, wet skin, and the smell of sunscreen in the air, Anya dropped her big news on me—she was about four weeks pregnant. Jake was the father (of course). The blessed event occurred on week twelve, the day the fans voted for her to do a sex tape. Oh Jake and his unwrapped snake! I'm sorry but in this day and age, there is no excuse for unprotected sex. She said that once they broke up she stopped taking the pill; of course, when they got back together the pill takes a few days to kick in and Jake hated condoms, blah blah blah! First, they have broken up a million times, so why she would decide to stop taking it I cannot imagine. Second, 98% of all men everywhere hate condoms. Who cares? Y'know what they like more than condoms? Sex. So the choice is pretty freakin' easy. (I made that statistic up, but I'll bet it's pretty accurate.)

I asked Anya right out whether deep down she wanted to get pregnant; she said she wasn't sure what she wanted. If the fans found out she was preggo the site would be over; dumping Jake to the curb didn't involve having sex with him.

Rules are rules and the fans, especially the fringe, would not let this pass. We could pretend that the deed was done before Jake had been voted off the island—women have been lying about when they got pregnant for centuries—but I didn't like the idea of turning our project into one of those teen pregnancy type of reality shows. We were so much better than that.

The only real choice was an abortion, but I knew better than to say that to Anya directly. That is not the kind of decision any girl wants to be pressured about, especially if she knows that the person pressuring her is trying to protect a website. I said that no matter what she decided, I was there for her (which was true) and I told her that she didn't have to make up her mind that day. We could wait and see what the fans picked for the next makeover and take it from there. If the fans wanted her to take drugs or do something else that would endanger a baby, Anya would have to make a decision. She could not do a makeover that hurt a fetus unless she was sure she wasn't going to keep the fetus. We just had to cross our fingers and hope that the normal fans would win the day.

When we got back to the apartment, Anya crashed on the bed but I stayed up so I could see the winning choice. It was a close call, Marijuana and Molly were only a few hundred Likes short, but the winning makeover was participating in a Native American Sweat Lodge. Hungryhawk2151 uploaded this cool video about the history and meaning of the Sweat Lodge Ceremony and some of the amazing epiphanies he had in the past and I guess it swayed the fans. The ceremony also includes the passing of a sacred pipe. You're supposed to "load" it with all of your hopes and dreams and then when you pass it around and everybody smokes it, they kind of smoke your hopes and dreams into fruition. Something called *kinnickkinnick* (my new fave word!).

The whole thing sounded très cool—kinda like a hookah minus the tar and nicotine. Not a bad way to drop a few more pounds either. Because Anya loves all things spiritual—tarot card readings, homeopathic medicine, getting your chakras cleansed—a Native American ceremony was right up her spiritual alley. It looked like we would get the break we needed until I read that "pregnant women are not advised to participate."

To tell or not to tell, that was the question. Anya had gone through too much to end the project just because of Jake's preference to ride bareback. But it was her decision.

I slept on the couch (barely) and the next morning got up and did my warm-up walk (5 min) followed by alternating 1 ½ minutes of jogging and two minutes of walking. Sounds boring, right? Sometimes Bryan went with me, not because I need security (obviously) but just to get out of the apartment. Jogging with Bryan is a mixed bag, especially with him constantly straining to see behind every bench and tree. The problem with paranoia is that it's catchy—by the end of a run I felt nervous every time we rounded a corner.

Although Anya grew up in a house that is practically right under the Hollywood sign, [Picture of Anya's house (mm35a)] her mother is a true southern girl and raised her with the saying, "When in doubt, pinky out." No joke. She can't help it. Iced tea, coffee, Red Bull, diet soda—she lifts a glass or a can and the pinky goes up too. And it doesn't only happen when she drinks something—she could be holding a tofu burger, a cannoli, or a fork loaded down with spaghetti.

One of the fans started an album on the site and uploaded any picture in which Anya looked particularly lady-like. The funniest one was a picture of Anya when she was sixteen eating a pulled-pork sandwich before she went veggie: sauce all over her face, barbequed pork falling out of the bun, and there's her pinky, dripping red, sticking up into the air. In my American Lit course the professor also posted discussions asking about foreshadowing. I always thought that this was strictly a writing device; I didn't think they naturally occurred in real life. I guess anyone who has written a memoir starts to notice that along the way there are warning signs, but most of us are too busy living to notice them.

When Bryan and I returned to the apartment, I made a goat-cheese and broccoli omelet sans the food that makes breakfast fun—English muffin, home fries, and fruit. Anya got out of bed and had a bagel and cream cheese (In general, I can put up with skinny girls as long as they don't complain about looking fat.) I told her about the Sweat Lodge. She was thrilled (do I know Anya or what?) and relieved that she wouldn't have to take any drugs. She asked me some questions about what we should wear (baggy clothing), where the ceremonies took place (California, Pennsylvania, New Mexico, Nevada) and whether we should eat before (a little). I printed out FAQ pages from various websites. On one of the pages the topic "Pregnancy?" was listed as a hyperlink, but to get the information she would have to go on the internet. She took the pages into her room and I waited.

Signs warning pregnant women are posted about every ten feet at Disney World but it was unlikely that there would be anything like that outside a Sweat Lodge. Of course, if she planned on having the baby, I had a moral obligation to tell her, but what about my obligation to the site? I decided to let the universe decide (to use Anya's New Agey thinking). If it wanted her to have a healthy baby it could easily steer her towards that hyperlink about Sweat Lodges and pregnancy. And if she was truly considering having the kid, she'd do the motherly thing and Google and see the same cautions that I saw.

Anya came out of her room carrying a bag and wearing workout clothes. We had until midnight to announce our decision about whether we would accept the makeover but Anya wanted to do it right then. My stomach twisted into a huge knot. I asked her if she had made any decisions about the baby. She said no, she wasn't even sure what she was going to say to Jake, if anything. I told her that we had gotten calls from HBO, and *Modern Family* was interested in having her on for a guest appearance. Of course, if the web site was closed down, their interest in her would shut down too. Either that or they'd make a joke out of her.

Actually, no one from *MF* had contacted me, but I was pretty sure that they would be up for it. Anya never missed that show; as an only child she got a kick out of seeing the way the siblings (both young and old) squabble and compete for attention. I told her that in real life it's not that funny, but I guess that's the point of the show. We have enough real life in real life. She left for her Hot Yoga class (shouldn't yoga be chill? I mean, how much sweat can you work up stretching and breathing?) and Bryan and Tommy went with her. I was alone in the apartment—well not really alone, Jake the Python with his cold dead eyes would keep me and my guilt company. I slipped from my low carb/no fun diet and made a huge bowl of garlic mashed potatoes.

Why I Love Potatoes

I love them anyway they come—mashed, diced, baked (once or twice), whipped, scalloped, broiled, fried and distilled (vodka!). Fun fact I learned from a Snapple cap: Potatoes have more chromosomes than humans. Of course, another Snapple cap said 50% of all Snapple cap facts are false, so who knows. Either way, I have always felt that I was destined to love potatoes: when my mother was carrying me she craved them so much that she would be too impatient to cook them—just peel and apply salt. Her first time around with Maren was hard; she vomited for seven of the nine months; her only craving was to hold down her food, any food. Even now, after everything, she smiles when she remembers her easy pregnancy with me full of starch and salt. This has always given me a stupid sense of pride. But that day, my fave comfort food gave me no comfort at all.

Usually, I would take a taxi over to our production office. Yes, we have an office now and yes, I can use a taxi anytime I want and call it a business expense (yay!). I hired this young, very "New Yorkish" woman, Rachael Stewart, to oversee the interns and Sam and Jon, our IT guys. (PS: It is really cool to be the boss of people who are older than you.) Because I needed to have a bathroom within five feet, I decided to stick close to the apartment, so I called and asked Rachael to put the interns to work comparing airline prices and hotel accommodations for northern California. The mashed potatoes weighed a ton in my stomach, bubbling in my belly like quicksand. I ran to the bathroom (again!) and out spewed a white river of hot vomit. (**No Picture—you're welcome**)

I told myself that this disgusting display was due to my stomach's shock at coming across so much starch after weeks of only protein, but maybe my body was punishing me for my betrayal of Anya. Or it could've been fear about my own makeover (butter, sour cream, milk and cream cheese—how many pounds would they put back on the scale?). One thing I can say for sure, I will never be able to look at garlic mashed potatoes with affection again. ☹

Anya came home and told me I looked like hell, which I'm sure was true. She put me to bed in her room and brought in some green tea. If there was one thing I didn't need right then it was Anya being thoughtful. Just looking at her made my stomach churn. Plus, unless I'm eating Chinese, I don't like green tea. But I said nothing. What I did do was call Jeff Morton Productions (thanks IMDbPro.com) and left a message that we wanted to discuss a possible guest appearance for Anya on *Modern Family*. They might not be interested, but I knew someone there would call back because *makemeover.us* carried quite a bit of clout. Bryan said that there was a small group of fans and paparazzi hanging around the exercise club entrance. We either had a leak or we were being hacked. We decided to go old school: from that point on, no specific locations or decisions on categories would be texted or emailed. Face to face only.

On the plane, Anya looked as cool as a cucumber and I was a hot mess. I didn't even order a drink from the flight attendant, which is a good indication of how disgusting I felt. I hadn't eaten since the mashed potatoes and had lost 4 pounds (BMI 21.5). I decided to tell myself that I was fasting for the ceremony. We landed in the Met Oakland International Airport, and as we made our way to baggage, it occurred to me that Anya actually had an entourage—the film crew (Javier, Austin, Dave) security detail (Bryan, Tommy, Joe) Make-up (Cathy) and Production (Leanne and myself). We chose to take one intern with us, so they picked straws and Leanne won. As we waited for the limo (I should put that in quotes because it looked like a regular van—très disappointing), I got a call from the *Modern Family* production office; they were very interested, so we set up a phone conference for the following week—at least that little lie wouldn't turn around and bite me.

The interns found us a penthouse suite that had five bedrooms, a sunken living room, small kitchen and a big deck with a grill and an outdoor Jacuzzi. Even though I felt like crap, I couldn't help thinking—*my first penthouse suite!* The guys took about two minutes to dig out their bathing suits and fire up the Jacuzzi. Bryan didn't go in though—he wanted to scout out the hotel and surrounding area first. Javier wanted the girls to take a turn, said it would be great video, but Anya wasn't into it. Because she was planning on having the baby? Because she doesn't like Jacuzzis? I didn't want to ask. Dave broke out his ukulele and Tommy slapped some steaks and chicken on the grill with a few veggie kabobs for Anya. We looked like a happy group, but I didn't feel a part of it—the information I kept inside made me an outsider.

10 PM. Anya was out on the deck talking to Jake on her cell. By the time she got off the phone, everyone else had gone to their various rooms. I think the boys were playing a little poker, but Cathy and Leanne crashed early (Well, not that early—in NYC it was 1 AM). Bryan had the pull-out couch all fixed up and was reading the manual for operating the Jacuzzi—he said it helped him relax. He wanted to sleep on the couch so that he could face the sliding glass doors that led

out to the deck. Anya locked the deck door behind her but I knew Bryan would have to check it at least five times before morning.

She came into the bedroom and started putting on her pajamas. I couldn't stand it any longer.

I said, "Well?"

"Well, what?"

"What are you going to do about the baby?"

"Why is that any of your business?"

"Seriously? Look around! Your life is our business! Everybody in this suite is employed because of your business."

"Fine. I'm having the abortion."

"Oh. Okay. When did you…"

"Decide? About ten minutes after I found out I was pregnant. I'm eighteen and trying to make a comeback. Having a baby right now would be crazy."

"Then why didn't you tell me?"

"First, I haven't even told Jake. Plus, you've changed. I wanted to see how much."

"Oh, really?"

"About a month after we started at H--------, I needed to leave but I still had one table who hadn't paid yet. They had just given you two parties, so I asked you to grab the tip for me. Three guys in suits. Ordered the wings—extra hot. Remember?"

"Sort of. You wanted to go to that midnight movie with Jake, right?"

"Yeah. Anyway, I had waited on these guys two times before that. Liked to tip 50%."

"Cool."

"I wanted to see what you'd do. Take all of it and claim they stiffed me or just shave a little off the top."

"I gave your book to the manager. If you didn't get the whole tip, it wasn't me."

"I know. It was all there. That's when I knew I could trust you."

"So what are you saying? That you can't trust me anymore?"

"Pregnant women and sweat lodges are not a good combo."

"So you knew."

"You should've told me."

"Your problem is that your whole life, everybody has given you anything you wanted. Star role on a TV show. Rich parents. College whenever you get around to it. As soon as something gets hard, you want to pack it in. I'm sick of holding your hand and convincing you to stick with a project that was your idea."

"And your problem is that you think the site is more important than anybody or anything. So when it came down to risking a baby or risking the site, you chose risking the baby!"

"You're the one who decided to get an abortion! You decided your interests were more important than the baby. How come it's so bad if I do it?"

"Because I'm the one who has to live with it after."

"You're a selfish bitch, just so you know."

"And you're a sycophant. Look it up."

I looked it up. It means somebody who flatters people to get ahead. I had just called her a bitch (see previous rationalization for not categorizing bitch as a swear) so how could I be a sycophant? But she meant that I was fake, and I guess she was right. That's the biggest thing I'm trying to work on now—and it's harder than most people think.

Sweating It Out in the Lodge

As we got into the van to drive us to the lodge, I told Jav and Anya that I wasn't going to take part in the ceremony. I am not the spiritual type and with things being so bad between Anya and me, I just wasn't up for it. I thought it wouldn't be a big deal, but I was wrong. Anya said that if I didn't do it, she wouldn't do it. She liked using her power to make me do things—it evened the score a little.

There were over a hundred fans and paparazzi at the Sweat Lodge—somebody was definitely leaking info, but who? Unless there was a tap on my cell. (Greetings, NSA!) Javier wasn't allowed to get footage of the actual ceremony, but afterwards the sweat lodge leader did allow us to interview him about the history and purpose behind the ceremony. Javier showed the hut, the fire, and the stones and taped Anya at the feast. A few other participants talked about what they got out of the experience, although some of the people were kind of offended that we were there.

They felt like some things are too sacred to be commercialized and I get why they feel that way. Jav wanted to interview me but I said no because I was still too freaked out. I did some major hallucinating in that torture chamber. Maybe it was due to the "fasting" I did before the ceremony. Since then I have read that some veterans have tried experiencing the sweat lodge as a way to let go of some of the demons they are struggling with. Maybe we should've encouraged Bryan to try it. But entering the subconscious is a tricky business; you never know what you'll find there.

They pour water over rocks that have been heated in a fire, which as you can imagine, creates a hellishly hot steam. On the rare occasions when I go to a gym, I never use the steam room or the sauna; I figure that one of the benefits of civilization is that we have developed technology and materials to AVOID extremes in temperature; deliberately putting myself in a room that is over 100 degrees seems masochistic to me. And if I did have to put up with extremes in temperature, my genetics are geared towards cold rather than heat.

About two hours in, Anya's face looked wavy; her features changed and she began to look like my sister. Anya/Maren's face started to melt and the room started to swing from side to side. Inside my head I screamed but it I don't know what it sounded like when it came out. The leader kept saying that there was a darkness trying to get into the lodge. He kept waving his hands into the direction of the opening in the hut, making a *shooing* type motion. He said it couldn't get in because the lodge was sacred, but he warned us that it was not gone for good. He looked at me when he said these things—at least I think he looked at me. It was murky as a womb in there.

Some people talk about how cleansing it is, but there was nothing inspiring about it for me. Maybe my subconscious is dark and terrible and that made my experience dark and terrible too. In her interview, Anya said she had an epiphany about *divine timing.* I don't believe that everything is decided by some all-knowing God or Universe; I think a lot of people use the *Universe* as a placebo for disappointment.

Week seventeen was finally over and we were once again safely back in New York. I am down to 135 pounds, BMI 21.8. I had until Week 23 to lose another 4 pounds, which would be a piece of cake (get the pun?). Anya made an appointment at a clinic somewhere out in the suburbs—she didn't tell me which one—because they offered a VIP treatment that guaranteed privacy. Jake was going with her. In the old days, I would've argued against Jake going because if any of the paparazzi or fans followed them there, it wouldn't be hard to put two and two together. I would've gone with her instead. But she didn't ask me because I didn't have the right to share a tough time with her anymore. All I had was the website.

Chapter 18

Heartache

Week Eighteen

My mom called—my father had been admitted into the hospital that morning. Apparently Dad has had angina for years, but they never bothered to tell me. He was outside cleaning the gutters and felt a squeezing sensation in his chest. (Unfreakingbelievable! Why didn't they hire somebody? They live in the retirement mecca of the world.) He took one of his pills (nitroglycerin—Jeez!) but the symptoms didn't go away, so Mom called 911. I asked Rachael to keep an eye on everything and packed some bags.

Rachael called Anya and she turned up at the airport to see me off. She told me not to get buzzed on the plane because I would need to be sober for my mom. All of a sudden I felt very cold and my body started shaking—although my mom didn't say the words, I could tell my father had had a heart attack. Anya put her arms around me until my body stopped shuddering.

"Everything's going to be all right," she said firmly. Then she thrust out her hand and extended her pinky. "Pinky swear."

I smiled. Of course she couldn't guarantee anything, but it was nice of her to pretend. I extended my hand and we linked pinkies and shook. "Pinky swear," I replied.

One of my dad's arteries was blocked due to some plaque that had ruptured; by the time I got there they had already done the angioplasty and put in the stent. (Thanks, *WebMD*) I drank one Bloody Mary on the plane (It's like a mini-breakfast when you're on the run—tomato juice and celery. The flight attendant carded me but luckily she didn't match my fake ID with my plane ticket.) I did take Anya's advice and only had ONE rather than my usual two on a short flight and three on a cross country.

I took a taxi to Tampa General and located my dad and mom in recovery. My mom said that they do heart transplants there, so an angioplasty is a piece of cake to them. I have to say that my mom was doing great. She was all business— taking notes on what my father could and couldn't do in the five days after the surgery, what he could eat, what symptoms to watch out for. She hadn't seemed this *awake* in a long time. I yelled at my dad (sort of) for not telling me about the angina earlier and for climbing a ladder in the middle of summer. He said that he did these kinds of chores early before the heat got to be too much. So what's that? Like 5 AM? This was Tampa.

My mom said that if I wanted to jog the next morning she would make me a map of the neighborhood (like I would be up before 8:00 AM). It turned out that she had been following the website, had "Liked" Anya's new hair color, had voted for a miniature pig for a pet (which would've been awesome but too much like *Honey Boo Boo*) and thought that the whole Sweat Lodge thing was "a fool's errand." She didn't vote on any of the options for making me hotter because she said I was attractive enough, but did like the idea of me exercising regularly and limiting my sugar consumption (Just say no to Type 2 Diabetes).

Dad got released the next day (yay!) and we dusted off some of his favorite games from the BTA period—Scrabble, Checkers, Dominoes. Maren was a big fan of Scattegories but that game did not make it to Florida. My mom and I went grocery shopping and bought all kinds of fruits and grains— exactly the opposite of the low carb diet I am on. We had turkey burgers for dinner (disgusting) and egg white omelets for breakfast (if it doesn't have the yolk, how can it be classified as an egg? What we were really eating was the unborn chick's placenta sans salt to make it edible.) My mother posted a heart healthy menu on the fridge for each meal for the next two weeks. Snacks included animal cookies (9), Melba toast crackers, and canned peaches. Seriously? Why canned?

She threw out every high cholesterol item in the house—goodbye butter, the hard cheeses (cheddar, parm, mozz), Pepperidge Farm Cookies, bacon, peanut butter and all types of chips. When they first found out about the angina, my mom had gone through every cabinet and filled a garbage bag with boxes of processed junk, but over time my father had replaced most of his favorite snacks. Like me, he has a weakness for food that tastes good. I don't know if my Dad's attack jarred my parents awake or if they had been slowly coming back to life down here where the humidity is always between 95 and 100 percent, but they seemed stronger than they used to be. It felt like they weren't listening to you through a haze of white noise.

Day two at my parents and I checked the website—no announcement of a category. I called Rachael but got her voice mail. I had been trying to resist going on Facebook, Twitter and Tumblr (out of respect for my dad) but by 2 PM that day I couldn't wait any longer. Twitter was exploding with rumors of Anya's abortion. Well Women's system had been hacked and links to an exterior security camera's footage of Jake and Anya walking into the clinic were all over the place. The fans' YouTube channel was filled with "normal" fans and members of the fringe making accusations and suggesting theories. I finally got a call from Rachael; she said Anya had barely come out of her room.

Even though she made the decision pretty fast, I'll bet it wasn't easy to walk into that clinic and go through with it. Just because a woman uses her right to choose doesn't mean the choice is easy. I happened to know that Anya did want to have children some day; not allowing it to happen must've felt horrible. In the old Puritan days they used to shame people by putting them in stocks in a public square. All day long your neighbors could humiliate you and you were literally defenseless. Of course, now we have the internet for that. Anya refused to even think about a category.

She hit puberty while she was still on *Extra Points*, so her chemistry was all screwed up between the dieting and the gymnastic workouts. After the series was over she got into other substances, which messed up

the normal functioning of her body even more, so she wasn't one of those girls who was never late. She was late every other month. And sometimes she didn't get it at all. So we stopped worrying about it. I guess we thought that if she did want to get pregnant someday, she'd probably have to work at it. Do the infertility treatments. I'll admit it. I was relieved when she said she didn't want to keep it because one thing I knew was that I didn't want to be like my father. I know a lot of guys say that, and then turn out exactly like their dads, but when I have a kid, I'm going to be there. Not just for the first few years or every other weekend—I am going to be a major part of that kid's life.

And that probably wouldn't have happened if Anya had decided to keep the baby. Which is why I wasn't against the abortion. I get that the guy doesn't have the same say as the woman, but for Chrissake, she told Rhiannon before she told me, which still gets under my skin. Who did she ask to go with her to the clinic? Who held her hand while the doctor did what she had to do? Whose shoulder did she cry on after? Not Rhiannon or any of her other "friends." When she's in trouble she turns to me. It was true then and it's true now.

This Week's Category: "Damage Control"

Day 3 – Breakfast consisted of low fat yogurt sprinkled with flax seed (poor Dad) and half a banana. I booked an early flight back to New York and called our IT guys and had them put up messages on the site and throughout the social media universe with the following talking points:

1. Anya had exercised her right to choose.
2. This was a private matter.
3. As a longtime friend, Jake had accompanied Anya, but he was not the father and had no connection to the pregnancy.
4. Anya had arrived at this decision after much thought and hoped that fans would respect her feelings and her privacy at this time.

At first I was tempted to have the IT guys distribute a denial that the guy with Anya was Jake because the images from the security cameras were grainy and Jake had his head bent. [Picture of Jake and Anya entering the clinic (mm36ab)] But you can really see his profile in this one. [Another Security Cam Pic (mm36c)] I couldn't take the chance that some paparazzi with a photo lens the size of my arm might have a picture we hadn't seen yet. The fans could speculate all they wanted, but the procedure was done and the DNA was gone, so unless Jake opened his big stupid mouth, we could ride this one out.

I put a call into *Dateline*. Their format would allow us to make this about a woman's right to choose rather than whether Anya broke the rules of the website. With states trying to shut down clinics (I'm talking about you Texas), if we handled this right, *makemeover.us* could be more than just an online freak show.

When I arrived at the apartment, there were about two hundred people outside carrying signs and chanting slogans. The police had even put up temporary barricades. Some of the pictures on the anti-abortion signs were truly disturbing-- babies with severed heads and legs. One woman carried a picture of Anya on one side and Hitler on the other; the slogan below said that they both killed the innocent. I called Jav and told him to get lots of footage of the Pro-Lifers, especially their gruesome signs. [Picture of disgusting sign (mm37a)] I was hoping that this would arouse sympathy for Anya, who had to walk through this gauntlet. We needed all the help we could get. Most popular tweets from the Pro-Life faction went like this: "At #makemeover.us headquarters to announce the truth to #Anyathebabykiller about #abortion. #Murder is a sin, not a choice." The president of the NARAL was giving it right back. The whole thing made me want to eat a quart of Super Fudge Chunk Ice Cream.

I called up to the apartment and Bryan escorted me into the building. Anya drifted from room to room, sometimes going over to the windows, but I don't think she was looking at the protesters below or anything else. Her parents had called and from what I gather they didn't appreciate hearing about their daughter's abortion on *CNN*. They were Baptists and didn't just go to church, they lead Bible study groups on Tuesdays and Thursdays.

My first reaction was CNN??? Who would've thought two months ago that CNN would cover our little website? Austin was channel surfing when he paused on a journalist from one of the local news networks interviewing Jake. She asked him whether he was the baby's father. At first, Jake stuck to the script, but then he said that a lot of fans had misunderstood his relationship with Anya and he looked forward to giving his side of the story someday. He also said that "certain people" who surrounded Anya might have pressured her into aborting the baby "for their own selfish reasons." He was now officially Jake the Douche in my book. Obviously he was putting the word out there—meet my price and you get my story—and I knew exactly who would come off as the bad guy. If it were a matter of money, we could've probably matched any offers he might get, but I was pretty sure that watching from the sidelines wasn't good enough for him anymore. He wanted his fifteen minutes along with the money.

I needed someone to persuade Jake to keep a low profile. Anya couldn't be counted on—she and Jake were no longer talking because he tweeted something stupid to some girl (shocker!). Anya felt that the least he could do after the abortion was NOT flirt with other girls on Twitter. I hate to say it, but my first thought was Bryan. Most guys are intimidated by him, especially since he got back from Afghanistan; aside from hiring the Mafia, he was our best bet. My cousin and I muscled our way through the protesters and went for a run (I will nail that 5K). I explained the situation and told him that I wasn't asking him to hurt Jake, just scare him straight.

When Bryan dropped by Jake's place he took his two Pit bulls with him and put muzzles on them so they would look even more dangerous. [Pictures of Bryan's dogs, Harley and Davidson (mm38abc). PS: Part of my deal with Bryan is that there would be no pics of him anywhere on the site. He was afraid that somebody might recognize him and track him down. Probably part of his PTSD. Of course, the paparazzi had taken tons of pictures of him anyway, but in his mind, at least we shouldn't be *supplying* them with either his personal info or his pics.] Bryan never specifically mentioned the site or the pregnancy; instead, he told Jake a story about a soldier in his platoon who ratted out another soldier. Loyalty was something the military took seriously because you had to know that the guy next to you would cover your back. If that person was working out his own angles, somebody could end up dead. He told Jake that once you enter the military, you never leave it. According to his rulebook, you sell out a friend, expect some major blowback. He said that Jake looked like he was about to crap his pants, so hopefully he got the message.

Back in the apartment, Jav and Austin decided to film our python eating his first meal. Pythons only eat about once every three weeks, which makes me wonder what they do to amuse themselves the rest of the time. Austin took Jake out of his aquarium/cage and put him in a box. (I don't know why but for some reason it's not a good idea to feed him in his home). He put this cute little white mouse in a plastic bag, which took forever because it kept biting Austin and running up his arm, then swung it around about fifty times so that the mouse got super dizzy. Then he placed the mouse in the box and in the blink of an eye Jake wrapped around his prey and waited for it to suffocate. It was surprisingly still in Jake's grasp, too disoriented from the ride in the plastic bag to defend itself. I told Anya about the appearance on *Dateline* and she told me that her parents were worried she was going to hell.

It was bad enough that she sent one of her security goons over, but Rhiannon went too far when she had him bring the Pit bulls. Anya knows how much I hate dogs. When I was about four years old, this friend of mine lived at the end of the street. My mom used to make my older sister, Karen, who was probably about fifteen back then, walk me down there. When we had to go by the Peterson's house, I used to get scared because they had this big dog, and it always barked its head off when anyone came close. Every time I used to beg my sister to carry me, and every time she reminded me that the Peterson's had an invisible fence and the dog couldn't hurt us.

So one day we were walking along and the dog started barking like crazy and running towards us. We both stopped and waited to see the dog run right up towards the edge of the yard and then back off. Something must've gone wrong either with the fence or with the dog because that day it bounded right out of their yard and straight towards us.

My sister knew it would be stupid to try to outrun the dog, so she picked me up and pretty much wrapped me around her head. The dog came at her and started tearing at her leg. She couldn't even kick it because she had me grabbing her neck like it was a life preserver. The Petersons were home and heard us screaming. Mr. Peterson ran into his garage, grabbed a shovel, and hit the dog until he let go of her leg. Karen didn't put me down until he dragged the dog back into the house. When my mom brought Karen home after the emergency room, I hid in the closet of my room. I didn't want to come out because I thought that Karen had turned into a dog. I asked my mom if she had to wear a leash now. Everybody got a good laugh out of that. I'm glad I didn't tell that part to Anya.

Having an ex-military thug talk to me about loyalty while he's got a couple of muzzled Pit bulls was below the belt. I'm not the one who needs to hear about loyalty. Why do women have to tell their friends every goddamn thing? It's like they debrief each other. Anya didn't realize it, but every time she talked about me, Rhiannon would file that information away so that she could use it against me later. Everybody wants to know why I cheated on Anya. Like she'd end up with a guy who lays tile for a living. I'm just the post rehab dude she's slumming around with. I knew that once she got back on top, she wouldn't remember my name. Before Rhiannon's goon came around, I was planning on breaking it off, beat Anya to the punch. People think ex-junkies are easy to push around. They think we're weak. But anybody who's gone through withdrawal and stayed off the stuff is one tough bastard. Compared to that, dealing with a couple of Pit bulls is nothing.

Chapter 19

Back to Basics

Week Nineteen

Our numbers had gone down, partly due to the abortion thing (the religious fans were very disappointed in us) but mostly because of the rumors regarding Jake. If the fans didn't believe that the makeovers were real, we were sunk. If that wasn't enough, other websites blatantly copying our format were beginning to surface. One was MakeMeSweet. The concept was to put a woman who tends to be a bitch into frustrating situations and force her to behave like a civilized person (lame!).

This week's category had to be something the fans couldn't resist. The site had achieved its popularity because people like the power of making choices that physically affected another person. We needed to tap into that again and quick, so we chose the category of "Piercing Anya." Immediately a bunch of makeovers were suggested: some typical (eyebrow, tongue, lip, nose, and belly button) and some less typical (snake bite, nipple, corset). [Pictures of different types of piercings (mm38.5abc)] My old boyfriend, Miguel, the one who worked at the tattoo shop, also did piercings so before getting my tat of Goofy he pierced my tongue, but I kept tapping it against my teeth, which drove him crazy, so I took it out. Because my parents didn't seem to notice the tongue piercing, a few weeks later I got Goofy. I'm not sure whether they noticed and weren't up for the fight or whether it just didn't register on their radar screens. They obviously had more important things to think about, but I kind of wished they had said something. Anya was nervous about the category because of the fringe makeover suggestions (Genital—yuck! Definitely not putting an example of this up!)

Luckily, she had something else to think about—her audition for *Steel Drums*. Rims Productions sent over a script and it looked like a cool project; however, I thought that the girlfriend part was predictable and one dimensional, so I asked them if Anya could audition as one of the drummers in the band. They could make her a stud lesbian and keep a lot of the same character traits. This took a lot of guts on my part because A) Anya would've taken whatever they offered, and B) have I mentioned I am just barely an adult who can't even drink legally!!!, but I had a feeling that we could do better and I went with it.

Rims said they were willing to give it a shot, so we set up the audition for the next day. Anya flipped out when she heard the news; I hadn't seen her this happy since before we started the site. She hugged me and whispered "thank you" in my ear. We spent the rest of the day picking out what she'd wear and running lines for the scene. I wanted to make her appear tough enough to be a stud but sexy enough to make guys wish she wasn't. We were two friends again, hoping for that big break in a business that chews young women up and then spits them out like old bubble gum.

Leaving the building the next day was a nightmare—PETA got on our cases for Javier's video "Feeding Jake the Python Snake" (boy can they mobilize quickly) and began protesting right next to the Right to Lifers. We had to make our way through this sea of bobbing poster boards of dead babies and tortured animals. Majorly depressing. Bryan, Tommy, and Joe helped us part the crowd and get into a waiting taxi. One of the paparazzi got too close and Bryan shoved him to the ground. The dude pulled out a knife, can you believe it? Some of these paparazzi are former felons, I swear. Bryan just laughed and taunted him to bring it on. The paparazzi took one look at Bryan's war tats and backed down.

Anya started freaking out in the cab about what kind of crowd would be waiting at the Rims Production offices—she's never been the same after William Stanton Mitchell. I told her not to worry—there's no way the fans knew where she was going this time. I had followed our new communication plan; there would be no digital info on our location for hackers to hack. Even the taxi company didn't know our destination; we told the driver what streets to take and he took them. The old interns had been let go and the new ones had signed contracts and were given limited details. All that hassle was worth it because when we got to Rims the sidewalk was empty: no paparazzi, no protestors, no fans. (Yay!) Anya NAILED IT! At least, that's my opinion. Patrice Hamilton, the show's director, seemed to like her in the role, but we'll have to wait and see if an offer comes in.

Lana Jordan, the creator of MakeMeSweet, actually called me with a job offer; she said that if I were smart I'd get out now while the site still had some users. Between the religious right and PETA, we had offended both the left and the right and the middle wouldn't stick around for much longer. She said her site was gaining every day (which was unfortunately true, I looked it up) and could use a strong producer who would "take them to the next level." I told her I would think about it. She said that I shouldn't think too long.

The winning makeover was…Corset Piercing – go figure. Corset piercing is when a bunch of rings are inserted into your skin so that you can be laced up as if you were wearing a corset. Why someone would want their skin stitched up when you can buy a cute bustier is a mystery. I guess they think it's edgy and sexy. The next day we bought some light blue ribbon, drank way too many shots, and went to Wildside Tattoo on Broadway and got Anya her corset. [Picture of Anya getting her corset piercing (mm39a)]

Please note: I would've liked to have shown more pictures of Anya's piercing rather than just this one, but one of our psycho fans keeps hacking the site and deleting the corset shots. The only picture he (or she) is willing to leave up on the site is the one where they marked her back with a Sharpie before putting in the rings. Why he/she is okay with leaving this shot up, but not the rest, I have no clue. It's one thing to suspect you're being hacked but it's another when there's actual proof. It is really creepy, like going back to your apartment and finding out you've been robbed. Some stranger has been sifting through your stuff, deciding what to do with it. It's even worse when you know that this person could come back anytime and destroy anything. And based on what? Some crazy obsession that you can't figure out. It gives them so much power. I've asked Jav what we can do about it, and he's looking into hiring someone who specializes in security. Sigh. It's times like these when I almost wish I could go back to waitressing at H------.

Anyway, the next day we bought a sweet dress with a very low back to show off the piercing and went to a sunset cruise/fundraiser for public television. Our clip of Anya at the fundraiser was also hacked, so no link to that either. Thank God our hacker only had this one fetish or there would've been nothing left on the site! When we got back to the apartment, Anya and I passed out in her bed (I made sure she slept on her stomach to avoid irritating the piercing) and the guys found random spots in the living room.

About 4 AM I got up to pee and nearly stepped on Jake (the python). I screamed because it was nighttime and I really hate snakes. Bryan jumped to his feet and pointed his gun at me. He yelled, "Drop to the ground!" I didn't recognize his voice. It sounded inhuman and scary. I seriously wanted to drop to the ground, but I couldn't because the snake was down there. I didn't know what to do—he kept yelling "Drop to the ground, drop to the ground!" I got down on my knees, hoping that would be enough, but he yelled, "All the way down!" The idea of putting my face right next to a snake horrified me, but I went all the way down because Bryan scared me even more.

Joe turned on the light and yelled "Dude, it's okay. It's Joe. You're not in Afghanistan! Chill! You're at Anya's." Bryan kept standing there, aiming his gun at one person and then another, unsure of who was an enemy and who was a friend. In response to the light, Jake slithered into a corner; Bryan saw the movement and fired. The snake jumped from the impact of the bullet. Bryan fired again and caught the snake in mid-air. One thing was for sure—Bryan knew how to handle a gun.

Shooting the snake seemed to settle him down and after a while he apologized for threatening to kill me. He looked like a kid who got caught shoplifting a candy bar. I told him it was fine; he was just doing his job, which was true, but inside my bones quivered like oatmeal. Having Bryan around is reassuring in some ways and disturbing as hell in others. We found Anya hiding in her closet. Thank God she couldn't find her cell to call 911. We all went out to the balcony and Dave plucked away at "Over the Rainbow" on his ukulele. Austin rolled a joint and each of us had a few hits. Except for Anya. I had to give her credit—she wouldn't touch a blunt, even after being rattled by gunshots. I'm glad people are finally changing their attitudes about weed; sometimes the only thing to do is hide behind some smoke and wait for morning to come.

The next day Patrice Hamilton called and said that everybody loved Anya's audition and wanted to discuss a contract. Up until that point, I had pretty much cock-blocked any agent who wanted to represent Anya because I didn't want anyone else telling her what to do and what not to do. And she seemed okay with that after Epstein's rejection of her audition. But we needed someone who knew how to negotiate a deal, so I asked Rachael to put some feelers out. Anya wanted to meet a *friend* for coffee, but despite Bryan's threat, I wouldn't be surprised if she were meeting Jake.

My Take on Love and Sex

I know I'm young, but I don't understand the difference between love and addiction; they both seem driven by hope and spoiled by disillusion. By eighteen, most girls have had sex or at least a serious boyfriend, but I haven't had either one. So far, I can't seem to dive into the sea of love the way other girls do. I guess I'm afraid the currents will pull me down and drown me. I only go out with guys who are NOT pushy when it comes to sex. Miguel looks like he'd be macho and domineering with a girl, but he was super sweet. We did some stuff, but we didn't go the distance if you know what I mean. I just couldn't get my body to go there.

After four months, he got tired of waiting (he was twenty-one) and started talking to this girl he worked with. Once I found out about him and Nicole, you'd think I would've attacked him on Facebook and Twitter or at least threatened to beat up the girl who stole him from me. I know girls who stalk their old boyfriends and go out with his friends just to get even. It's weird that I didn't do any of that, but I guess it didn't bother me that much. Like I said, when it comes to love, I'd much rather stay safely on the beach and just dip my toes in.

But there was no fighting Anya's determination to see Jake, so Cathy turned her into a blond, Tommy escorted her out the back of the building, and I crossed my fingers that the fans wouldn't find out. I yelled at Javier and Austin for not securing the top of the python's cage but they both swore they had been very careful. None of us said it but we all wondered if someone had broken into the apartment while we were on the cruise and let the snake out as a prank. The manager of the building stopped in and said that he didn't want to be a jerk, but rules were rules and we had broken quite a few of them. (No exotic pets, No discharging firearms (seriously there was a reference) and No undue disturbances (the protestors).

We had until the end of the month to vacate the premises, so we decided that it was time to go *all in* and buy a place with enough rooms for all of us and a little guest house that would function as our production office/editing suite. It would have to have a gate and private road to ensure that the paparazzi kept their distance. Bryan and the guys would have a great time setting up a security system—hopefully there would be no more leaks and no more pranks.

Jav and Austin took the snake to Dave's parents' house and buried him in their backyard. (Note to PETA: Jake was given a dignified burial. We did not flush him down the toilet as some of your members insinuated.) I hired a PR firm to release a statement about the accidental loss of our snake and Anya's role in *Steel Drums*. Twenty-four hours later PETA promised an investigation. (Sigh).

Anya started getting weird packages and letters during week three. Some of them were sweet (Literally—in a video clip Anya mentioned that she loved pistachio fudge and we received five pounds of it.) This woman (brooklynchick479) started uploading a haiku on the site every day—but they stopped coming in around week eight which is too bad because some of them were pretty good. Did she get bored? Find some real life girl to write poetry for? Develop a crush on another celebrity? This was the last one:

> Auction starts with flair
> Bids for breasts, a nose, some hair
> Watch her disappear

@KnittingKnut849 sent in an adorable eggshell colored hat, kind of an oversized beret, that Anya actually likes wearing. [Picture of Anya wearing beret (mm40a)] In an interview on E! Anya was asked who her favorite actress of all time was and she said Audrey Hepburn, and after that fans sent her lists of places in New York that were showing Hepburn classics (*My Fair Lady, Charade*), which was hilarious because Anya meant to say **Katharine** Hepburn (*Philadelphia Story, Guess Who's Coming to Dinner.*) Actually Anya is not a big fan of Audrey Hepburn; she thinks she is good, but too easy to love—like frozen yogurt on a hot summer day. She says that most teenage girls like Audrey and Marilyn but completely overlook Katharine who is a more talented and more complex; she didn't accept average effort from herself or anybody else she worked with and chose rolls that had strong outspoken women (*Adams Rib).*

But I happen to know (Film History 231, Screwball Comedies, Class, and Gender) that in her personal life she let Spencer Tracy pick her up and throw her down like a yoyo. Maybe Anya connects with her because Hepburn was raised in a wealthy family too, or maybe she understands that combo of strength in her professional life and weakness in her romantic life. One thing's for sure, from Doris Day to Rihanna, Hollywood women have always had their Jakes.

After that we had to videotape her attending some of Audrey's films just to keep the message on target, which was a bonus for me (who can NOT love *Roman Holiday?*). But some of the packages/letters Anya received were disturbing. Week Five a manila envelope came with one of those cardboard paper dolls wearing a camisole and shorts. It had shoulder length black hair like Anya and a tattoo was drawn on the shoulder. It didn't have any feet, which at first seemed accidental because the paper doll was old. The next week we received a cloth doll mailed from the same part of the city with a hole cut out where the heart should be. Obviously, a missing heart is not a great message. The following week we received a plastic doll that had blood dripping from its eyes, nose, and mouth and the word *FAME WHORE* written in animal blood (we tested it) on its belly.

What makes me mad is the arrogance. First, how many people in our society are NOT obsessed with fame? Look at all the reality shows and magazines about celebrities. And what about all the award ceremonies—there's like one every month almost. We're all fame whores. Those weirdoes who sit in dark rooms constantly trolling sites, looking like crackheads—they think they have the right to judge me and Anya? And where did this psycho get the animal blood, that's what I want to know. This is the kind of thing PETA should go crazy about rather than what happened to our pet snake. Bryan began confiscating Anya's mail and hired some veteran buddy he knew who was a bomb/ricin specialist to examine all packages before they were opened.

Chapter 20

Free Fall

Week Twenty

Anya started taking drum lessons and I was down to 134 ½ pounds, but we were losing our audience. We had to do something dramatic enough to invigorate our fan base while attracting new ones. I told Anya that if she wanted to keep HBO interested, we needed to keep our numbers high and that meant we needed her to do something edgy. We announced the category "Anya Gets Adventurous" with the following requirements:

1. The adventure could not be life threatening.
2. The adventure would be eliminated if it required training Anya did not have previously.
3. The adventure had to adhere to the law.

We offered examples: Suicide is not legal and is obviously dangerous; therefore, it could not be considered a viable adventure. Climbing Mount Everest (unlike ordinary hiking) requires skills in endurance and technique that Anya does not currently possess; but a guided hike to the base camp would be fine. The fans seemed to like the category, and makeovers poured in. Some of the popular suggestions were sky diving, African safari, swimming with sharks, bungee jumping, spelunking, heli-skiing, scuba diving, and zip lining in the rainforest. An adventure that was obviously submitted by the fringe and quickly rejected was "Walking on Hot Coals."

The winning makeover was "Sky Diving" Awesome right?! Sky diving is a legit adventure, and it would make great video. I could see Jav floating at 12,000 feet shooting Anya falling through the sky. What I didn't know was that Anya was deathly afraid of heights; she couldn't even go on a roller coaster. She was okay with flying in an airplane as long as she didn't get a window seat and took her valium, but sky diving was not an option. She said she would've been happier with the hot coals. It was a "no." Period. I told her this was her chance, her opportunity to make a mark, to guarantee her future. Seize it or forever regret it, but when someone is deep down afraid there's no reasoning with them.

During our visit in South Carolina at the Allens' home, Anya and her dad would sit on their porch (or should I say veranda! So southern!) and play chess in the late afternoon. At first it looked incredibly boring, but after a while I found it fun to watch them try to out maneuver one another. I told Anya to think of this project as one big game of chess. She was the king, the one that had to survive for us to win and I was the queen, the second in command, the one who was ultimately responsible for protecting her; Jav and Austin were knights and Bryan was a bishop. Our opponents were everyone who wanted to take us down—the media, the fringe, other actors, copycat websites. Protecting her was the same as protecting myself; the best way to stay in the game was if I made the jump.

Javier could shoot her participating in the ground training and getting into the plane. I would go through the training as well but off camera. The trick was making me look enough like Anya so that Jav could film me in the air. We would have to have everyone sign confidentiality agreements. Anya knew that if the fans heard about the switch they would blow up the social media landscape, but if we were careful we'd make it to next week, which was Fans' Choice—a category they loved.

For her, the series on HBO was a lifeline; it would be her chance to prove she had gotten her issues sorted out, that she should be taken seriously as an adult actor, but my feelings were mixed. It was fine for Anya to go off and film *Steel Drums* as long as we could keep our numbers up. But we couldn't afford to lose her unless we had a replacement or some new direction for the site. As the queen in this game of chess, I had to be ready to make some sacrifices and one of them might be her role on *Steel Drums*. Hopefully it wouldn't come to that, but if it did I crossed my fingers that in the long run she would thank me.

We found out that even with lessons, the first time you Sky Dive you can't go solo; you have to ride tandem style on your instructor's back. I had imagined dramatic video clips of Anya (me) doing a few somersaults, holding hands in a group in the shape of a heart, but that's only for advanced divers. I am a Swedish chick and have the big bones to prove it, so despite losing 8 lbs. (hurray!) I am still a couple sizes bigger than Anya, so Cathy and I had to figure out what clothing Anya/me would wear. The hair was no problem (short black wig), I could wear goggles to hide my blue eyes (one of my best features I'm told), and we could get a temporary tattoo. Luckily, with Anya's implants, my boobs wouldn't be an issue.

The instructor's name was Emilio and he had calves that would make any girl hot (Given that I haven't had any action in the romance department for three months, that was très easy to do!). Which brings me to my limited use of the French language. It's true, I can recall only about six words from my high school program and most of them are adjectives or adverbs (très, petite, sans). I have two full sentences that never left my brain—"Ferme la bouche" (Shut your mouth) and "Je ne sais pa" (I do not know—which I used way too often in discussion posts in my French II class with Ms. Blanchine). I developed a love for randomly inserting them after seeing *Breakfast at Tiffany's*.

Okay, Anya's right that Audrey is easy to love with her pointy face and tear drop eyes, but she is a crème brûlée, not a frozen yogurt, with a shell that was harder to crack than most people thought. *Breakfast at Tiffany's*—that line about getting the mean reds—I first heard it when I was sixteen and if you don't know the quote look it up because it's awesome. Maybe all teenagers go through the mean reds; puberty is a horrible stage of life. Either way, some trends are worth bringing back.

Six hours later and Jav, Dave and I were ready to dive into the sky with cameras strapped to our bodies and instructors attached to our backs. I have to say that although butterflies crashed against the lining of my stomach as if they were on meth, it was A-FREAKING-MAZING. Seriously!!! I laughed and screamed at the same time. (An embarrassing side note—I am pretty sure I peed my pants a little on the way down.) I wish Anya could've experienced that feeling—sans the peeing of course.

Unfortunately, when we landed, somehow despite Emilio's guidance, I hurt my ankle. More of a strain than a sprain. No cast needed, but I swore a blue-streak. As a guidance counselor, my mother was against using curse words; she felt they were the mark of a person with a small imagination or inadequate vocabulary. She had to hear it at school and didn't want to have to put up with it at home. Exceptions were only allowed when a person was in sudden pain, such as the stubbing of a toe. She got me into the habit of not swearing and in general I hardly ever do. But my ankle was killing me.

When I tried to get up from the jump (as Anya) I couldn't put weight on my foot, which made Emilio kneel down on his muscular calves and inspect my already swelling ankle. Unfortunately, this is where we got greedy. It seemed like an opportunity too good to waste—Emilio bending over Anya, an over the shoulder shot of her face scrunched in pain she was bravely trying to hide. It might even put the fans in a more sympathetic mood when they chose the category next week. We could get Anya some crutches and she could hobble around for a few days. It turned out that Emilio also wanted to be an actor (who doesn't??) and was definitely up for more camera time. At the time it seemed like a good plan, but of course it blew up in our faces. (Heavy, heavy sigh. I just read this sentence back.)

When we got back to the apartment (after a stop at the walk-in medical which took forever) Rachael and the interns were busy packing Anya's kitchen for the move. Jav, Dave and Austin went straight to the downtown office to transfer the footage so they could start editing. I discovered pretty quick the downside to our plan for pretending Anya had a busted ankle—I had to pretend I did NOT have a busted ankle. I could not use crutches in public and could not even be seen limping! Plus, I had 1 ½ pounds to lose and a 5K to run in two weeks.

We found a place to live that is less than an hour by train to NYC but I am not putting up a picture or even giving the name of the town for security reasons. Bryan was helping one of the interns (Felice) wrap and pack the dishes. I think he has a thing for her, which is cool because she seems like the low maintenance type. He vetted our new group of interns and Bryan and Felice discovered they were from neighboring towns in Connecticut (he's from Hamden and she's from New Haven). He was less fidgety when she was around, and she didn't get freaked out when he checked the locks for the hundredth time. So hurray for young love even though I haven't even made out with a dude in forever!

Bryan asked if he could have a couple days off so that the two of them could go to Mystic Aquarium (they both like beluga whales). [Picture of a kid they saw kissing a beluga whale (mm41a)] What he really wanted to do was introduce Felice to Aunt Jody and show her off to his friends. I told him GO—we'd still have Joe and Tommy to escort Anya to her drum lesson. I was determined to lay low and order a pizza (Don't even start with me) when who texts me but Emilio! Naturally, I had to wonder—did he want to get together because he was attracted to me or did he want to get together because I am a producer and he is an actor who is looking for future work? The thing was I didn't care. The idea of a guy interested in my contacts rather than my cup size was très cool!

I hopped into the shower, which brings me to another stupid issue I have had to deal with as producer of this nuthouse. Now that she was famous again, it was only natural that Anya felt the need to spoil herself with some expensive bathroom products. Every girl's dream is to spend hundreds of dollars on body lotions and scrubs that make her smell like a heavenly paradise filled with flowers and perfumed waterfalls. While I am more than happy with my Suave body gel, Anya had spent quite a bit of time finding just the right combination of lotions, scrubs, and talcs at S---- and did not appreciate it when her Lavender Apple Body Wash was nearly gone after just a few uses. Like The Three Bears, she knew that someone had been sampling her body soap.

Naturally, I was her first suspect; she figured that my Ocean Breeze body gel wasn't cutting it. I had no problem defending myself—all she had to do was sniff my skin which smelled like cheap chemicals rather than an aroma derived from natural ingredients like rice and corn. Her next suspects were Cathy and the female interns; we had to be careful questioning Felice because if Bryan sensed any accusation against her he would freak the hell out. Nevertheless, Anya's body scrub was also very low and her body lotion (enriched with avocado and olive oil) was almost gone after only one week. Both of us didn't want to consider the possibility that some jerkoff was sneaking into our bathroom to shower with Anya's products.

That night the apartment was almost empty—Anya and Joe were at drum practice and Tommy, Jav, Austin, and the IT dudes were playing a couple hands of poker. Anya's place has become a communal hangout which kind of sucks for Anya. This is why we need a house with a *separate* guest house. I showered with my standard Ocean Breeze wash and shampooed with my Herbal Essence Body Envy (my hair tends to be bone straight and anorexic thin) and got ready to meet Emilio at a nearby sports bar (no locations—sorry—I was underage at the time!). I told him that it was very important that he didn't tell anyone about where we were meeting because it's hard enough to lose them, I didn't need them getting inside info. (Yes, the paparazzi had begun to follow me too. It was glamorous for about thirty seconds.)

I will summarize this encounter with one word—Ugh! You would think that a guy with those calves who is not only a struggling actor (a dime a dozen in NYC) but also a sky diving instructor would be interesting, but you would be wrong. My body said yes, yes, YES! but my brain said WTF!

Joe came back to the apartment sans Anya—she decided to go to a *friend's* place and wouldn't need him for the rest of the night. This was the second time since Bryan's warning and it was obvious that Jake had successfully wrapped his reptilian body around Anya's life again. Maybe, despite his flirty tweets and sleazy Instagram pictures, he did love her— any guy who was willing to risk bodily harm from a vet with two Pit-bulls must've been in pretty deep.

I met Emilio and had a personal pizza, (I told myself I would only eat half of it) but the conversation didn't get off the ground (he's a sky diving instructor—get it?) I have learned to be a good sport about dumb blonde jokes (Speaking of dumb blonde jokes and pizza---A blonde was at a restaurant and ordered a pizza. The waiter asked her, "Do you want it cut into 6 pieces or 12?" She said, "Oh, please cut it in 6. I could never eat 12.") Therefore, I do not automatically think that just because a dude is muscular and handsome, he's got nothing up top in the brain area. However, all he wanted to talk about was weight training, sky diving, and acting—three subjects I was sick to death of. He was so boring I ate the whole personal pizza.

When I got home the guys had just come back from playing basketball and were sitting in the living room waiting their turns for the shower. I can see hanging out here during the day, but coming here to shower is a little much. Judging by their lack of sweat, it looked like Jav and Austin had already had theirs—but something was up; they were acting suspicious. My first thought was that they had smoked some weed and felt bad for not waiting for me. I plopped down on the couch next to Austin; one whiff and I knew that the smell I was getting was no weed I had ever experienced. I leaned really close into Austin's chest and took another sniff. Apple-Lavender. When the apartment was empty, these dudes liked to try out Anya's scrubs, lotions, and talcs!

And, being guys, they poured out handfuls of it rather than the dime-size portion suggested on the backs of the bottles. I couldn't resist kidding Austin about his girly smell, so he pinned me to the floor and made me say "You are a manly man!" three times. For the first time I started thinking that Austin might actually have a thing for me. But I just can't see him as anything but a friend. That's the problem with women—we always want the guys we can't have. Austin was sweet (literally!) and he looked out for me, but when I thought about who I wanted to make out with for a couple hours, it was Javier.

I was trying to figure out how to get Austin off me when the buzzer sounded. I thought most likely Anya and Jake had had yet another fight and she would come in either crying or swearing. Tommy went to the intercom and a girl's voice said, "Delivery from Big Apple Florist by Blakely." A lot of fans had sent flowers to Anya due to her *ankle injury*. Usually the service we hired to examine the mail took care of the deliveries too, but it was late and everyone was tired. Tommy went down to get them and the next thing we heard was a loud boom.

Looking back, I can't believe we didn't wonder why anyone would deliver flowers at 10:20 PM. Tommy did the right thing—if he had buzzed her up who knows how many of us would've been injured. We called 911 and ran downstairs. Blood was everywhere. Seeing it in person is so different from seeing it in a gory movie or even watching news footage of a terrorist attack like the Boston Marathon. I can only say that I am glad it was at night because the darkness hid much of the horribleness. Tommy's leg was in pieces but at least he was alive. We later found out from the police that it was Haiku Girl. She had put one of those pressure cooker bombs in the bottom of the basket but was so nervous about activating it that she didn't even look to see whether a man or a woman had come out of the building to pick up the flowers. (Can you really learn to make a pressure cooker bomb on the internet? Seriously?)

When the police asked Haiku Girl why she did it she said that she used to watch her on *Extra Points* and couldn't bear to witness Anya slowly destroying herself. She called it a mercy killing. We texted Bryan the next morning and he and Felice were at the hospital in just under two hours. It was hard for him to go into Tommy's room, but he did it. He knelt on the floor next to the bed and cried. Tommy was awake, but groggy. He touched my cousin's head and tried to say something but the words were garbled. Bryan said it had been his responsibility to train Tommy and he had failed. He felt he should've been there that night and couldn't look at Felice. She was now part of his epic failure. A nurse brought some flowers in and I burst into tears. I guess she hadn't heard. Tommy's family came in (they had driven down from Vermont) and we all cleared out to make room.

For the first time I wondered why Tommy had come to New York. Probably not to be a security guard for a TV star trying to make a comeback. Later his mom told me that he had majored in criminal justice but found out afterwards that he didn't like working in a prison. Too claustrophobic. I assured his parents that we would take care of any medical expenses not covered by insurance, especially rehab. Co-pays, anything he needed. His dad shook my hand but of course what I said wasn't much comfort. His son's leg was gone. All that was left now was finding a way to recover from that fact. **(No pictures or video clips of Tommy or his injury. On the site we uploaded a statement but that was it. Privacy is the only gift worth anything in this industry.)**

At first we could not reach Anya, probably because she was with Jake and thought we would give her crap about it. I finally sent Rachael over to Jake's apartment to inform her in person. She was horrified. It must be hard to know that A) the bomb was meant for you and B) someone else lost a leg because the bomb was meant for you.

The fans uploaded some very sweet sentiments on Twitter and their YouTube channel and traditional media covered it with their typical empty empathy. We were numb. Bryan was AWOL. Our lives were split between visiting Tommy, medicating Anya, and hiding from the paparazzi. I bagged the 5K I had signed up for and drank a lot of White Russians (for protein).

Chapter 21

Busted

Week Twenty-One

We announced a week hiatus to deal with the police and be there for Tommy, and the fans respected our decision. It seemed that everyone was in our corner until Georgia127 (our not so favorite conspiracy theorist) started posting videos of me and Anya. It turned out that boring Emilio had been paid off by one of the paparazzi who had taken video of me walking into the sports bar. It is really really hard NOT to limp when you have a busted ankle and you can see me favoring my right ankle on the tape. Some dude coming out of a class caught Anya with his cell leaving her drum lessons and calling a cab and uploaded it to YouTube. Unfortunately, while she was trying to flag down a taxi she DIDN'T favor her right ankle. Georgia127 found it and juxtaposed both videos on the fans' channel with little arrows pointing to me limping and Anya not limping. She also had frame by frame examinations of Jav's clips of the jump and views of the back of my head (supposedly a few tendrils of blond hair got loose from under the wig) and measurements of my legs (which are longer than Anya's).

But the worst evidence was the **V** on my arm. Cathy had applied make-up over it, but at some point that day the make-up must've come off. So that day the **V** stood for *Vendetta* because that is exactly what Georgia127 began. Doesn't this lady have a job to go to? If only Haiku Girl had sent *her* a basket of flowers. (That was really mean. Sorry Haiku Girl's mother! But I'm keeping it in because that's how I felt at the time.)

Chapter 22

The Shit Hits the Fan

Week Twenty-Two

The fans were furious and none of us had the energy to do more than take cover. I stopped looking at all social media, including YouTube, and sent Dave to get some Chinese food. (Screw the diet, bring on the noodles.) We would be crucified and cremated in next week's Fans Choice and the site would be over. Part of me wanted to yell and part of me wanted to crawl into a hole and hibernate until spring. Lana called and said that it was now or never—jump ship or go down with it. I told her to go f*%# herself

(Sorry Mom. In the movie business, dropping the f-bomb is about as common as drinking bottled water). I am not going to describe the media shitshow that followed—anyone with a pulse and an iPhone saw it. (If you did miss it, search Makemeover.us + betrayal + scandal or limp or tattoo)

Tommy was doing better, Bryan was still gone, Anya was surfacing from her meds, and the fans voted. The following category won by a landslide.

This Week's Category: Justice for the Fans

Makeover suggestions varied from the sane (a public apology/interview with Oprah) to the insane (multiple forms of suicide). Our numbers hadn't been that high since the abortion clinic videos were revealed. Most ordinary people like to see a celebrity fall from grace (I'm talking about you Lance, Aaron, and ARod!), and normally that includes me. But high numbers didn't make the people at Rims feel better, who were already regretting hiring Anya. *Steel Drums* would be a new series and Anya was supposed to bring in viewers, not alienate them.

Aunt Jody called and said that Bryan had talked to some recruiting dude about getting back into the military. He said that if he was going to be responsible for other guys getting their legs blown off, he'd rather do it in another country. My aunt thought that this was his way of doing penance. She also feared that deep down he was counting on tripping over an IED. Our only hope was that when they did the psych eval, they'd uncover his PTSD and refuse to take him, but given the army's need for experienced recruits and their poor management of paperwork, my cousin would likely be back in a uniform by next week.

The winning makeover was *Amputation of Anya's Right Pinky*. Yes, some fringe psycho had decided that the best way to take Lady Anya down from her pedestal was to chop off her finger. "When in doubt, pinky out" had a whole new meaning. The fans had included two requirements with the makeover: 1. Only local anesthesia could be used. (They wanted Anya to witness it.) 2. Three witnesses chosen by the fans would have to be present. Georgia127 was sure to be their first choice due to the role she played in uncovering the *Sky Diving Scandal*. The game was over, the jig was up, the tide had turned, you get the picture. We were through. Since the project took off, I felt like such a freakin' adult able to do all the things adults do—hire and fire people, rent an apartment AND buy a house, fly by myself, negotiate deals. I fooled myself into thinking that because I was doing those adult things I must have actually grown up. But that day I felt like a lost child.

Anya and I had a friend buy us three bottles of Dom Perignon as an ironic gesture and shared it with Rachael, Cathy, and the guys. (In terms of her sobriety, Anya put this down as a special occasion.) Bottle number 1: we toasted Tommy and Bryan. Bottle number 2: Anya. Bottle number 3: the website itself. With the dregs of the third bottle we anti-toasted the fringe by gargling with the champagne and spitting it out over the balcony. Unfortunately, I then switched to margaritas to drown my sorrows in tequila; I don't blame the Cuervo for the time I had to spend on our bathroom floor, I blame the salt and the lime because they dehydrate you. My old therapist used to yell at me saying that drinking was not an antidote for pain; in fact, all it did was create more pain, and I had to agree as I puked repeatedly in the toilet.

Anya's contract with Rims was not so airtight; our lawyers pointed that out to me a week ago, but I didn't pay any attention. I wanted the loop holes in the contract to stay open because I thought I might need them if we didn't get a replacement for Anya. I expected Rims to use one of those clauses—but no. It seemed that the people at *Steel Drums* were intrigued by the latest makeover suggestion; they were very hot on the idea of a female drummer with half a pinky. They didn't come out and SAY it, but basically it was this--if she doesn't do the makeover, obviously the contract was cancelled. But if she did do it, they would not only keep her but even increase her pay. They liked the idea of a "disabled female drummer breaking all the rules."

Suddenly, my mind cleared. Was it really such an impossible makeover? Could we find a way to keep the site alive for a little longer? If I could convince Anya I was pretty sure the rest of the crew would go along with it. After much thought, here were my talking points:

1. Tommy gave up a leg—the least she could do was give up a pinky.
2. We could probably save the pinky and attach it later.
3. Rims wouldn't include her in the series unless she did the makeover.
4. Tommy gave up a leg!

It didn't go all that great. Anya was horrified that I would even suggest such a thing. Her talking points were as follows:

1. She has cut and dyed her hair, endured painful procedures and allowed others to dress her up and

make her talk as if she were a puppet for long enough.

2. She is a good actress who should not have to cut off a finger in order to get a role.
3. Tommy did not GIVE UP a leg: it was blown off without his consent.
4. Despite articles on the internet, there is no GUARANTEE that a pinky can be reattached.

The thing that bothered me most was that we would be ending this project with a scandal, and we would be quitting in disgrace. After everything we had been through, our dishonesty would be the only thing that people remembered. Rims Productions would fall through, the paparazzi would find a new phenomenon, and our profits would disappear.

I promised Anya that if we did this last makeover, we would close the site and walk away with our heads held high. She would not only forever change her reputation, she would become a legend. We would get loads of interviews on any show we wanted. Make one final humungous score. She had to decide and she had to do it in the next six hours.

I wanted to get out of the apartment, so Joe smuggled me out the back door of our building and believe it or not I went to St. Anthony's on Sullivan. I'm on the fence when it comes to religion and had not set foot in a church for years, but I needed a quiet place to think. I always hear people praying to Saint Anthony for some THING they lost, but I heard somewhere that he is a finder of lost souls too. Bryan was lost and even though I have no idea what to think when it comes to God, Bryan seriously believed in all that stuff so I asked St. Anthony to protect him and help him find his way. I wondered if St. Anthony would think I was a lost cause for asking my friend to allow a doctor to chop off part of her finger. Did I even have the right to refer to her as my friend anymore?

The truth is I loved Anya but I also resented her. I wanted her to be happy, yet I did things that I knew would make her unhappy. Is that friendship? Another particularly crappy truth was I needed this project more than she did; before the website I had been like that green algae that sticks to the sides of a pond; I was afraid that without the site I'd go back to being that glob of goo. That's the thing about sitting in a church when it's almost empty—it's pretty hard to keep avoiding who you are.

Okay, so I followed her to the church. I wanted to get to Rhiannon without one of her goons around. Anya told me about the whole amputation thing and it blew me away. What kind of brainwashing bullshit was going on over there? I've set a fair amount of marble and tile in churches and temples all over the city. Still do it, though now I wear a safety harness. I don't care how dumb it makes me look. If I had worn it before maybe I wouldn't have slipped a disc and ended up hooked on Percocets. My doctor had me on it for about a year when all of the sudden—done! Wouldn't renew the script. Tells me to try ibuprofen.

Like taking a couple of Advils would do it. I went to another doctor, got another script, but maybe they all read the same article because no one would give me a script with more than two refills.

At first I tried buying them on the street, but laying tile doesn' t exactly bring home the big bucks. Same old story you heard a million times, I guess. Heroin looks like a cheap fix right up until you sell half the tile you got for the next job to pay off a dealer. Then you got to lie to the customers about damaged materials and word gets around. Finally you sell your tools because even when you get a job, you don't want to work anyway. Physical labor and heroin don't mix. It's just a matter of how many people you'll betray before somebody stops you, either with jail or rehab.

About a half hour later, Rhiannon came out of the church and I met her on the steps. I called her a parasitic piece of shit and a lot of other names I won't put down here. I asked her what kind of fascist organization she was running over there where an eighteen year old girl had to get amputated so that everybody else could get off without a scratch.

I expected a fight, but she kept nodding her head and agreeing with me, which sucked because that made it hard to keep yelling at her. Then she started crying and blubbering about how she was this empty shell before she met Anya. I'm not exactly sure what she said because like a lot of guys, I can't handle it when women cry. I either want to hit them or hug them. I kept searching my pockets for a napkin while she got it out of her system, but women take a long time to get it out of their systems. I said we should go get a coffee where there were plenty of napkins because people walking by were staring at us.

At Starbucks, once she got a hold of herself, I asked her if she was in love with Anya. That took her off guard, you could tell. Her mouth actually hung open for a second. She said she wasn't, that she had a hard enough time connecting with a guy. Girls have messed-up friendships—one day they're so close you couldn't put a cigarette between them, and the next day they can't stand each other. They'll even make out with each other just to see what it's like. All these months I had built Rhiannon up in my head to be this manipulative bitch but she's like everybody

else—trying to find a place in a world that doesn't want to make room for you.

When I left the church, who do you think was standing there waiting for me but Jake. Go figure. I'm not sure if it was a coincidence or what. Once I got back to the apartment, I told Anya that if she were willing to do it, I would do it with her. If the fans wanted someone to punish, they should punish both of us. I don't know if my offer persuaded her or if it was the invitation to attend the Emmys, but she decided to do it. I could see the footage in my head of both of us lifting our bloody pinky stumps in defiance. We would go out with a wow rather than a whimper. Say what you want, it would be unforgettable!

The crew was totally shocked, and at first Austin and Jav said they wouldn't be a part of something so twisted, but eventually they came around. We could do it without them, but none of us wanted to: we were a family (kinda) and needed to stick together. Rachael contacted our lawyer to see if we could, seriously, amputate a finger on national television. In general, if a person is caught trying to harm herself, authorities have to stop her because this is usually a sign of mental instability.

However, if a person is choosing amputation for a logical reason, then can the state argue that doing this indicates mental instability? And if it can be determined that the person involved is not out of her mind, does she have the right to harm herself? I put the word out to the networks (traditional and cable) but was pretty sure none of them would touch it. I called Dr. Leander and she promised to come over and give both of us psych exams—if she found us mentally capable then our lawyers felt we'd be okay.

Our PR firm wrote a response to the makeover and our plan to include my amputation. We stated that both Anya and I had conspired to betray the fans; therefore, both of us should participate in the fans' choice of self-mutilation. The social universe exploded. The fans were stunned that we had taken the makeover even further. All of that hate towards Anya and me magically turned into love. Of course, some fans were against it and begged us not to bow to the fringe. This created a mini-war between the two groups which made our numbers rise even higher.

My mom flew in from Florida with my Uncle Jack (she wanted some male support but didn't want to tell my father). I won't say kidnap, but I think she had this vague idea of scooping me up and taking me to a neutral place where she could talk some sense into me, and Uncle Jack was along in case she needed a little help with the scooping. Mr. and Mrs. Allen also flew in and they brought the family lawyer. They met with Dr. Leander and I'm sure they talked about the possibility of committing Anya. But Leander had already signed papers saying that Anya was capable of making this decision and Joe made sure that we had security around us at all times. (He had hired some new guys, but I miss Bryan and Tommy.)

Because we were legal adults, our parents had to beg rather than threaten, but we stuck to our guns. I gave them copies of a few articles I found on the internet regarding the success of procedures involving reattaching severed fingers, although I did not mention the fact that time mattered—you couldn't keep a finger on ice forever. Mrs. Allen was pretty much hysterical, but after Maren's death my mother was cried dry. I guess she learned to pull a wall over her features and hide behind it from my dad. For some reason that day her expressionless face really pissed me off. I totally went off on her.

I told my mom that if she had done even a little bit of parenting, maybe I wouldn't be talking about amputating my finger. Maybe I'd be on summer break from some really cool college rather than producing a website that attracts freaks who leave bombs on our doorstep. I told her that it was a little late to start pretending to care about me now. That was a low blow and I shouldn't have said it, but I got what I thought I wanted. My mother broke down and cried. She made these barking sounds that sliced through me like a chain saw. I thought Uncle Jack would literally kill me. He yelled at me and told me I was selfish and cruel. It made me wish I had a brother who would yell at someone who was hurting me.

You'd think after I put my mother through that horrible scene, I would've backed down and promised not to go through with it. But I still couldn't live with the thought of closing down the site in disgrace. Dr. Leander wrote out a script for a sedative for Mom and I booked them into a hotel. In the taxi, I tried to explain to them that losing a finger was nothing to me, especially HALF a pinky. What do pinkies do anyway? I was making a smart business decision—one that I would never regret. My mother's face had settled into that wobbly expression people wear when they are barely holding it together. She made a garbled, choking sound, but she didn't start crying again. At that moment, I didn't regret making her break down. I thought maybe she needed to do it. Too much holding in of emotions isn't good for anyone. Look at my dad—don't tell me his angina thing didn't come from repressing his feelings. And even if she didn't need to break down, I needed to see her do it. I guess my uncle was right about me after all.

On a positive note, after scolding me about the finger issue, Aunt Jody informed me that the army is not as lame as I thought and had found Bryan's previous paperwork noting his PTSD and were not accepting him. (Yay!) I texted Bryan's cell and begged him to please come back; we needed his protection now more than ever: these new security dudes were only temps! I reminded him that we never found the wacko who sent the packages with mangled dolls; plus, we still didn't know how our info was hacked. He agreed to come back. I hope I did the right thing by guilting him into it.

We contacted a few reservations and found a tribe who agreed to allow us to tape the procedure there. We wanted to be sure that police wouldn't barge in mid-chop. (That sounds like I didn't take the amputation seriously, but it was easier to act as if the whole thing was no big deal.) Native American reservations are technically separate countries with their own laws; I was pretty sure that forbidding a couple of white girls from cutting off one of their fingers wasn't a top concern. The fans had a vote and the three witnesses would arrive tomorrow at noon. We had to move fast because the Allens would definitely try to find another doctor to examine and commit Anya. Rachael chartered a plane for us that would hold our crew, a doctor, nurse, anesthesiologist, the witnesses, security,

and a few reporters and journalists from both traditional and non-traditional media platforms.

Jav asked our parents if he could interview them and get their reactions on tape. Both sides said no, but Uncle Jack agreed and he didn't hold back on what a dumb mistake he thought both of us were making. Jav was also able to interview the witnesses and get their take on watching the upcoming amputation. I personally texted Charlotte (previously known as @mebecraze) and told her that NO WAY should she have part of her pinky removed. Then Jav interviewed both Anya and me to record our pre-amputation jitters.

Anya and I talked about how we should handle the interview; we decided to go with a version of good cop/bad cop. She talked about her fear of heights and how bad she felt for trying to get out of the Sky Diving makeover. She was agreeing to this amputation so that she could live with herself for betraying the trust of fans who had given her another chance and supported her. I, on the other hand, basically flipped off the fringe and said I was doing it to show them I wasn't afraid of their psychotic revenge. Our hope was that members of our audience who had initially connected to Anya would love her all the more, while the fans who never liked Anya but enjoyed messing with her would be sidetracked into screwing with me. Twitter, YouTube, and Facebook buzzed with admiration and contempt and the media covered all of it with reckless abandon.

Day of Reckoning

It was strange meeting the witnesses. Georgia127 looked like my middle school social studies teacher—twenty pounds overweight, short brown hair, pleasant smile, sensible shoes. This was a woman who scanned the skies for drones with the same intensity that she examined our videos for fraud. It must be hard living in a constant state of suspicion. Rob from RobnSue was another witness, and he also looked kind of harmless—short gray hair and glasses. I think he secretly hoped we would find a way to fake the amputation. The third witness was a guy who owned a shooting range in Arizona; pretty much his whole upper body was covered with tats and he kept sharing his philosophy on how to solve the immigration problem—some kind of huge Taser system that would be twice as effective as an electric fence.

Bryan arrived just before we were supposed to leave. If possible, his eyes were more haunted than before, but the important thing is that he turned up. After we landed, Rachael had hired one of those luxury mobile homes to take us to the reservation and serve as a home base on the reservation. Anya was very quiet; I am pretty sure Dr. Leander, who had kindly volunteered to accompany us, increased her meds for this trip. Austin asked if I wanted something—a beer, a joint, a Percocet—but I said no. I didn't want to dull my senses; I wanted to feel everything. My body was vibrating with adrenaline. I understand now why some people do extreme sports—they want to feel alive, and one way to do that is to put yourself in danger.

At the reservation they had set up a make-shift altar for us to use. Jav set up his cameras, Dave attached lavalier mics on everyone and did sound checks, and the witnesses chattered nervously. Anya stood clutching Dr. Leander's arm. It occurred to me that Anya might not be able to go through with it. I tried to go over and talk with her but she kind of ran away as I approached. For me it was just a pinky, but for her it was losing one more piece of herself. She had been living at the mercy of the fans for too long and today was one compromise too many. I think Leander was definitely considering changing her diagnosis on Anya's mental state.

Finally, the altar was covered with plastic sterile sheets and a surgical tray was prepped with instruments and dressings. I say "finally" because time had slowed down to a crawl; we had to get this done before Anya fell apart completely. Looking back now I think that there are certain moments when we either live up to our highest selves or we don't. Obviously, I didn't live up to mine. I should have called it off. There was no excuse to put her through this kind of misery. But I didn't.

It was decided that Anya would go first because I seriously doubted whether she would submit to the amputation after seeing mine. Anya got herself together and moved away from Dr. Leander. She walked over to the altar with slow deliberate steps. We all held our breath. The doctor asked her if she was sure she wanted to do this and she nodded. He said he needed to *hear* her say it. She opened her mouth but no words came out. She swayed and then fell to the ground. Bryan was there in a flash; he picked her up and carried her to the mobile home and Dr. Leander was right behind them.

We all remained standing around the altar, unable to move. The cameras were running; the reporters were torn between retreating to the mobile home to cover Anya or staying at the altar to see how I would handle the situation. Without thinking, I stomped up to the altar (no dignified walk of the sacrificial virgin for me, which is ironic because I am in fact a virgin) and slammed my hand down on the sterilized plastic sheet. I wanted to say something cool, but all I could think of was "Do it!" The doctor looked at me, at the anesthesiologist, at the nurse. He was definitely rattled by Anya's collapse. I didn't want to lose my nerve so I yelled, "You need me to say it? I give you permission. Now chop it off!"

He kept standing there, frozen over his surgical tray, unsure of what to do. He said something about not feeling comfortable with the situation, and I said something about the amount of money we had spent on his services. Not to mention the plane, which he would have to reimburse us for if he didn't do the job. I was talking tough but really I was afraid. I could live without a pinky; I wasn't sure I could live without doing this final makeover. I looked him in the eye and said, "Someone will get a pinky amputated today. Either you do it or I will." Maybe he saw the desperation in my eyes. I really did NOT want to have to amputate my own pinky, but I think I might've gone through with it. He nodded at the nurse and she sterilized my finger and then the anesthesiologist applied the digital block with a needle.

We didn't actually need an anesthesiologist because neither of us would be going under, but it made good video— the more medical staff there the better. After a few more seconds that felt like hours, Dr. Minkowski picked up a pair of scissors. (I imagined a saw or a scalpel, but for some reason scissors were more scary.) I tried to look bravely at the main camera; I don't know how it came across because I have never watched the video clips. I heard the snap of the scissors and even though my pinky was numb, I felt the loss. Maybe it was my imagination or maybe it was nerves, but I swear I felt it leave me. I didn't look down because as I have mentioned, I get nauseous when I see my own blood.

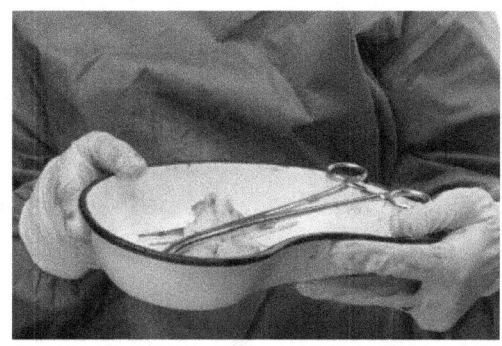

(Yuck! I don't know who took that picture. One of the paparazzi probably paid off the nurse.)

Come to think of it, these last few months have been filled with spilled blood—Tommy's, Anya's, Jake's and mine.

When they were done swabbing the wound and sewing the flaps of skin together, I lifted my hand to show the witnesses and the camera. The doctor's cut was right above the knuckle; the rest of my pinky looked so small as it was placed in a Ziploc bag and put in the cooler. **(NO picture of my amputated finger. Sorry. I have to draw the line somewhere.)** This wasn't the big ending I had imagined for the site, but it was the best I could do. The nurse gave me some pain killers but I held off taking them until after the interviews. First I had to see Anya.

She was propped up against some pillows, lying on a couch, drinking a glass of water. It was a combination of the heat, the meds, and of course, the fear that caused her collapse. She sucked in her breath when she saw my hand.

"I was going to. Really," she said.

"Shhh. Don't worry about it." I responded.

"I just kept thinking…" she stopped talking. The meds had definitely kicked in.

"I know. You don't have to"

"No, let me say it."

I let her say it.

"It's just that…I already gave up something." She looked at me right in the eye to see if I knew what she meant. I knew.

"How much more…I mean, at some point…a piece here another piece there… what happens when there's nothing left?" She gave me a small smile. "But I was gonna do it. Pinky swear."

We both looked at my bandaged hand. We couldn't help it. I went over and hugged her and she hugged me back. She hadn't agreed to the makeover to ensure her place on *Steel Drums* or for the fame—she had done it for me.

Later, a reporter asked me if the website was finished and I said yes. Even I couldn't ask Anya to keep occupying the center ring of my circus of crazy.

Strange Days

Most people, when they take pain medication like Vicodin or Percocet, feel sleepy or dopey; when I take pain meds it is as if I have downed three Red Bulls—every inch of my body quivers. The next few days following the amputation I was hyper-aware of everything and everyone around me. Jav and Austin were busy editing and uploading the footage, but when I did see them they acted weird: Jav wouldn't meet my eyes and Austin tried to avoid me altogether. Editors have to watch footage over and over again to find the exact angles and cuts; it must've been hard for him to watch the amputation so many times, especially the close-ups.

Rachael had her hands full dealing with the media's requests for stills and footage and interviews, and the interns were so careful NOT to look at my hand that they bumped into each other. I couldn't shake the feeling that everyone was watching me and trying NOT to watch me at the same time. I guess they seriously questioned my emotional stability, which I can understand now but didn't understand then. I had done what was necessary. Why were they treating me like a psycho fan? Probably the only person who talked to me as if I were a normal human being was my cousin Bryan; I think he would've given up a limb to take back that moment Tommy picked up the basket. He knew that I had to do penance and half a pinky was a bargain.

When the Allens found out their daughter had NOT gone through with the makeover, they were incredibly relieved and incredibly kind not to show it too much around my mother and Uncle Jack. Mom wanted me to bring the Ziploc bag to the nearest hospital so that they could reattach the finger. According to the web, if they operated during the first twelve hours after amputation, my pinky had a very good chance of complete rehabilitation. But then there would be no turning back, no eleventh hour CPR for my dying site, and that was a chance I could not take.

Anya called Rim Productions and told them that on the advice of her psychiatrist she was asking to be released from her contract. She informed them that the last few weeks had left her emotionally unable to handle the rigorous schedule of a television production. Anya told me that she was just sick to death of it all; she wanted to go back to South Carolina and find some small private college close to her parents' house and maybe that's the truth. Or maybe she knew that *Steel Drums* would cut her loose and she couldn't bear to be dumped by a show again. It's hard to know with Anya. Like every good actor, she instinctively keeps a part of herself hidden so deep that even she can't remember where to look for it.

The next morning Patrice texted me. I almost didn't look at it because I thought she was going to yell at me about Anya, but she wanted to know if I was interested in auditioning for the show. She said that they were all really excited about the idea of a disabled drummer and didn't want to rewrite the script. She wanted the show to cash in on the press I was getting. Acting has never been my thing, but then again producing was never my thing until Anya persuaded me to do it. I asked Anya if she would mind if I took Rims up on the audition. She shrugged and said no. She told me that if I wanted to ruin my life by becoming a television star it was my decision.

I read a short story in my Intro to Lit class (Pre-Req for my American Lit class) about this guy, Goodman Brown, who went for a walk in the woods and met an old man who was obviously the devil. Goodman Brown had just gotten married and he was crazy about his wife, Faith, so at first he stayed strong and refused to sell his soul, but the old guy kept showing him all of his neighbors who were going to this big bonfire to worship Satan. Goodman Brown got really depressed that so many of his friends had sold their souls, but he was a Puritan so giving into the devil was a major deal.

Then the old man showed him that his wife was going to be at the bonfire too. Seeing her there in her Puritan bonnet wrecked him, and he kind of passed out. The next day he couldn't figure out whether it really happened or whether it was just a crazy dream, but the suspicion that his wife was really a witch ruined their marriage. He couldn't respect any of his friends either. He was completely alone and you never know whether he was the only good guy in his town or whether he just thought he was. He pretty much lived a bitter and lonely life.

So, the question is—is Anya sort of like Goodman Brown? If I go to the audition, will she never be able to look at me the same way again? Am I like everybody else, willing to sell my soul for fifteen minutes in the spotlight? I think a lot of people have a black hole inside them. You can fill it up with pills or alcohol or some other obsession, but you can't leave it empty. I used to fill mine up with Lexapro and vodka, and after we left H------, I tried to fill it up with the website. But if the site was over, then what would I fill it up with? I just didn't know if I could turn down Patrice Hamilton and be like Goodman Brown. The thing is, the rest of Goodman Brown's life sucked because he felt that the devil had robbed him of what made him happy. But I'm starting to think that nobody can do that. Sure somebody can steal your cell or your purse, but I've been blaming everybody else for taking something from me and leaving a black hole when it's probably something I created in the first place. I guess the truth is, the person who really needs a makeover is me.